THE PACT

By

Brandon Reeder

This book is dedicated to my grandfather. As a kid, everyone tells you that you can be whatever you want to be when you grow up. I would just like to thank him for being the only person that I believed when they said it.

Eden

Eden Indiana is the kind of small town that makes you think you live in Mayberry with Andy and the gang—and at one point you even realize you have the whistle down. Friday nights are everyone's life here, even the adults. I mean it's either that, or meeting up at the local CVS to rev engines up and down Main Street with your buddies for a thrill. On the other hand, you could be in with the gangstas, who even have their own mini rap group complete with the marijuana. Any way you chalk it up, a kid like me is an outsider. Don't get me wrong, I can dig life in the fast lane, and nobody likes a party as much as me; it's just a motorcycle and hair like Nikki Sixx doesn't exactly fit in with either of those quality groups. It especially doesn't go over with the olden folk. My name is Cole Harris, and the story of how my life changed forever starts here, in Eden…

"Hey! You better be going to the party tonight Cole!"

"Don't sweat it Katie, I'll be there." This is your typical start to my Friday here at Columbia High. Katie is one of those girls who make you weak in the knees just hearing their name; you know, one of those beautiful girls where you lie awake at night just wishing you could be lucky enough to be the one she holds hands with. She also is a very sweet and accepting girl; probably the only person who has really tried to understand me in this crap hole…and she's also my ex.

"What up pimpin'? I tried to get a hold of you last night to see what's going on tonight but you didn't answer...so? Is it happening?" This was a typical greeting from my best friend, Tyler Moore. We had been friends since I can remember and ever since my mom passing and his dad's arrest we have always stood by each other through everything.

"Yeah man, I got Oxycodone, Trams, Xanax, Vic 750s, a quarter each, and enough alcohol to fuel a weekend at the track. You gonna be able to go? That leash is getting pretty tight isn't it?"

"Shut up man, Elaine doesn't have to know…"

"Right on brother, meet me at the lookout after dark and we will head up there, I got to get to math class." Tyler and I had developed what most people would call a bad habit. Over the years we became more and more rebellious, and walked the line of recklessness. Drugs are a norm for both of us, as well as fighting. I can't count how many times one of us has been broken while the other one super glued them back to new.

The stinging alarm of the bell awakes me to a detention and freedom until Monday. The mad rush to leave school is almost comical in its sense of chaos; like their lives will abruptly end if they cannot reach the doors at 3:21. I just go to my locker, get my leather jacket and keys, set my iPod to a little Rob Zombie, and walk towards my Harley. The Harley is a '67 hardtail with a new S&S motor powering it instead of a tired shovelhead, the peanut tank and frame are both powder coated black, and the tan leather hand tooled seat is one of a kind. As soon as I get on it at the end of the day, it's just me, two wheels, thirty minutes at fifty-five miles per hour, and 145 cubic inches of freedom in its purest form.

The sight of my grandfather's cabin is euphoric to me as I roll thunderously into the driveway. Living in the cabin I inherited from him had its downfalls, like the endless lists of duties to maintain it such as staining, mowing the immense lawn, and chopping wood for the stove, which was my chore tonight.

As I split my last piece of wood for tonight, the downpour begins. I guess it was a good thing I mowed the grass first. While putting away my things in grandpa's old pole barn, I glance at the clock and wonder how it can go from four to nine o'clock so quickly. That's the price I pay for inheriting a twelve acre lot with a wood heated cabin I guess.

Grandpa basically raised me once my parents split, and he had no choice but to take me in when mom passed in the spring of '08. He was like a father to me, especially when you consider I don't even remember much about my real dad. Anyways, grandpa and I were always close from the beginning. I helped him take care of the land in his later years; mow the grass and split firewood. So it was really no surprise when he left me the house in his will. Since I'm not married or enlisted, I couldn't actually have it until I was eighteen because of Indiana state law, but I think he knew the deep appreciation I have for the place—and for him.

Once acquiring the house, I had to show ability to pay property taxes, water bill, electric, satellite tv, all those types of amenities on a monthly basis. While I knew I could swing that money monthly, I couldn't exactly be telling government workers and lawyers that I buy and sell various drugs and make profit. So I had a friend get me a job at Alwen's Pit Barbeque, the local go to for good food and gossip. Within two months I had fallen into a managerial position and salary pay. When I wanted to accept, they told me the only way I could pull this off was to take my last necessary credit once a week in an online class through Columbia, I was even more stoked. So, the drugs slowed and the work ensued.

Tonight is Friday, however; and I have the night off for Katie's party. After getting a quick work out on the heavy bag in and grabbing a shower, I headed out the door to meet up with Tyler. This time, I trade in the hog for the diesel. I just bought her about a year or so ago after some good deals.

It's a 2008 Ford F-250 crew cab with an eight inch lift and beautiful 18 inch black rims wrapped in 38 inch Mickey Thompson bajas. The truck itself is white with black trim along the bottom. All leather inside with a set of 12" Kickers and a two channel amp, and the black smoke rolls out of a six inch exhaust with a nine inch chrome tip. I think it's safe to say that herb has been good to me thus far.

As soon as I pull in, Tyler, who was waiting outside, opens the door and hops in.

"You could at least wait until I put it in park next time, Moore."

"Yeah whatever pansy, just get us to the party alright?"

"Someone's grouchy; balls must be getting uncomfortable in that purse…"

"Well they happen to be out for the night so can we please just go get fucked up already?" Ty's relationship with Elaine could be described as strained, if you were being generous. They were the couple at Columbia who were envied from the outside, but all of their friends couldn't stand being around when they were together.

The constant fighting, head games, jealousy, and control is overwhelming to everyone close to them, myself included. I smiled and shook my head as he laughed at himself, and we peeled out of the parking lot and headed towards Katie's house.

The feeling of succumbing to extreme judgment upon arrival at a party could be one of the most awkward things ever. Especially at Katie's, where everybody thinks either we are going to get back together or Blake is going to kick my ass. Blake Johnson is her new boyfriend, and captain of the football team. And knowing how he feels about me, the whole kicking my ass thing stands a legit chance.

The Party was already hot by the time Tyler and I arrived. There were tables for beer pong, a huge bonfire, and the stereotypical groups congregating. The kids who were amateur at best with an instrument were playing for a reluctant crowd by the fire, the pretty girls were herded together watching the jocks do keg stands, and the few light weights were scattered around, passed out or puking.

After an hour of making my rounds of small talk, and smoking out my quarter with a friend of mine, Deon; I realized I had no idea where Tyler was.

"Yo, has anybody seen Tyler around lately?" I had made my way over to the bonfire by now, not that I was concerned about Tyler really, but on occasion he will get himself into trouble when he is partying.

"Hopefully he got the hint and left, and if he did it's too bad he didn't take you with him." Blake's taunting voice rang loud from the pond's dock. "How did you fuckin' posers get invited to this party anyhow? Because I know I didn't invite you, and Katie doesn't want you here either."

"Whatever bro, I just want to find my friend and then maybe we will leave; why don't you just go toss a football with your buddies or whatever it is you beer-bellied fucks do at these things." Blake was obviously drunk. He was slurring his speech and stumbling about as he shouted at me.

"That's enough both of you! Cole I'll help you find Tyler, but then why don't you just leave before something bad happens?" I always loved it when people said that after an intense argument. If a fight is so bad, someone please explain to me why we make circles around them and take videos when they break out in public. In any event, he went back to his keg and beefcake buddies, and Katie and I walked in search of Tyler.

"So you haven't talked to me in a week, and the first thing you say to me is get out?"

"That's not true, I believe I asked you to come to my party today."

"Sarcasm, nice."

"I thought so; you gotta admit it was kind of cute."

"Yeah, it was cute, but not kind of. Nothing about you is "kind of" cute."

"Well thanks I guess…where the hell is Tyler anyway? We are almost back to the fire and I haven't seen him anywhere." Subject changes like that hurt. I've broken just about every bone in my body and countless other things that people say hurt, but I'd rather go through any of that one hundred times over than to have her deliberately shun me away like that.

"Who knows where he ran off to, but thanks for walking with me; it's nice to get to see you once in a while. I better let you get back over to your fairy of a boyfriend though; it doesn't look like he is holding his liquor too well."

"Shut up Cole, just because things aren't how you want them doesn't mean you have to hate the world." Shocked by that response, I decided to sit down by the fire with a jar of shine. Not much after I get comfortable, I hear Blake shouting my name again.

"Cole! Hey boy, you still at my party huh?! I thought I told you to leave?" He was beginning to aggravate me, but I decided to just brush it off and ignore him.

"Sorry Blake, I'll get right on that pal."

"I ain't your pal you little rat. You think you're such a badass with your tattoos and motorcycle? You think you're gonna get Katie back from me? Well guess what? She hates you and she told me so." His shouting was drawing a crowd.

"Oh, did she tell you so? Damn, I'm surprised you remembered that. Now tell me, was that before or after you got your fifteen seconds of fame in that she thought about me?" The urge to give him what he deserved was getting harder and harder to walk away from. Blake just knows how to get underneath my skin.

"Don't interrupt me when I'm talkin', boy. Nobody likes you; you're trash. What would your mom think of you boy? Or even worse, your grandpa?" At this point, I was pissed off. Most of the time, I can just fire back with something witty and stingingly personal then laugh it off, but bringing up my grandpa was just a little too much to let go. So I ever so gently sat my mason jar down, grinned, and shot up from my seat by the fire meeting him full speed at the front of the dock and tackling him off the side into the shallows of the pond. I then got up and greeted him with two sharp lefts to the side of his face, and decided to just leave him to lie on the bank of the pond. I looked up to the stares of everyone there and then walked towards my truck. I stopped briefly in front of Katie, who was crying and looking at me like I had just committed first-degree murder.

"If your dick of a boyfriend is going to be at one of these next time you think of inviting me, don't. I can't believe you just sat there and let him say all that; you must really like seeing me in pain huh?" Katie looked at me with shock, along with everyone who had gathered to watch the showdown. It was quiet enough to hear a mouse, well, except for me. I was yelling; infuriated actually. How could she look at me like that? Like she was taking his side?

"Cole, I just…"

"Just forget it; I'm just a piece of trash so what's it matter anyway?" I walked towards my truck, grabbing a bottle of Jack and chugging along the way.

The Morning After

A bitter taste of alcohol, vomit, and the stench of last night awaken me to a chill early-autumn morning and the girl who was lying next to me. It was Jessica Matthews, a senior from the local all girls' school in the next county over. Jess is a nice enough girl---absolutely gorgeous too, so I woke her up and took her home on my way back to the cabin. As we rode together in silence, I couldn't help but think how I was helping add to a not so good reputation that Jessica had built up the past few years. The most bitter part about it is it isn't deserved at all. Jess is an honor student and well on her way to do whatever she sees fit in college.

As I watch her walk up her driveway, I can't stop thinking to myself how often this had been happening. Another party and another random girl that needs to be drove home in the morning. The guilt and shame of last night wash over me as I pull away and my mind shifts to what today will hold for me.

Since I did most of the heavy work yesterday, I decided to give my English Bulldog, Stanley, a bath. He is named Stanley because I think there is a little similarity between him and that big guy from the TV show, The Office. In any event, once he smelled all fresh I fired up the Harley and headed towards town for a joy ride.

Coming up on Main Street, I realized I was quite parched, and pulled up to Miller's, the local pub. While backing my bike into a parking spot along the street I could hear an argument going on behind me. Curious, I shut my bike off and turned around on the seat and was surprised to see Katie trying to get away from a group of six people. Four bigger scruffy-looking fellows and two old hags. Normally I would get up instantly and come to her aid, but with everything that happened last night between us, I was stuck in the mud watching.

"Can you please just leave me alone? You're all really starting to scare me!" Katie screamed. She was trembling in fear and trying to back away from them to no avail. Even so, I couldn't help but notice how amazing she looked. Her copper tan skin shimmered in the sunlight, and the simplicity of her pony tail, grateful dead t shirt, and jean shorts are as beautiful on her as any dress.

"Calm yourself sweetie, all he did was offer you anything you ever wanted. What's so wrong about that? A young girl like you has dreams I'm sure." Said the lady, who looked to be at least a hundred years old. She had wrinkles on her wrinkles, yellow and corroded teeth, and the most sinister looking smirk while looking at Katie. Come to think of it they all shared that smirk, which made me a little nervous for her. The six of them began to form a circle around Katie, and that cued my influence.

"Hey wicked witch of the west, Dorothy here doesn't like the bullshit your boyfriend is pitching okay? Oh and she isn't your sweetie. She doesn't swing that way trust me. As for the rest of you squirrely folks, the rape-like formation you are making around the nice lady here is concerning me. Kindly knock it the fuck off, thank you."

"Who do you think you are talking to us like that boy? You do realize there's six of us and one of you, right?" The biggest of the four goons said, trying to sound tough. He had a long braided ponytail, and a nasty unkempt beard.

"Well actually there's four dudes, but frankly I am more afraid of your women haas, they FUGLY."

"Boy, you made a mistake walking in here to play hero without any back up today."

"Uh oh," I went to the front rake of my Harley and continued. "Well lucky for me, I did bring back up." At this point, I unsnapped the buttons on my leather saddlebag and pulled out two throwers, one with a silver handle, the other gold. Pointing to the silver one I stated with a smile, "See this one here, I call it thunder, and this other one here, that's lightning. Oh and let me show you my best sidekick." I reached for the sheath on my back-left hip, and pulled out a bone handle knife with a Native American feather on attached to a leather wrist loop, not to mention a fourteen inch blade. "I call her the problem solver, boys. Now are you going to let the girl go or do you really want me to give all your beards a nice trim?" Suddenly the crack of a colt revolver rang loud and true causing everyone to look back towards the pub.

It was Addison Miller, a big name here in Eden, and the owner of this particular establishment. All the tourists who come through always think we named it that because everyone from here loves Miller Lite, but really the pub is named after Addison. He was a former baseball star who left Eden to go to law school at up state. He was the pride of the town before he left for athletics, and was surrounded by adoration once he returned. He's been back for about six months now, first starting out as a lawyer and now owns several businesses throughout the town. He was owner of the pub, a gym, and now owns the family practice where he got his start as an attorney. He told the goons to let Katie be and to return inside to their table; and with a serious and deathly cold voice told me to leave the pub and not come back. With that, Katie rushed to her car; passing me with a look of gratitude and disbelief in her eyes. I could have sworn by that look she was going to hug me and pour her feelings out or something, but she just went to her Prius and sped off.

Feelings of confusion and pain rushed my body, overwhelmingly. How could she just leave? Why did I even want her to stay? Somehow that girl just finds a way to keep me waiting; sometimes I think it's for something that will never happen. I stood there for a minute and watched her drive towards the horizon, and then buried the feelings and hopped on the bike to go home.

Home—there really is no place like it. This was my first thought as shut off the bike and walked up the drive towards my barn. There is a simplistic beauty about the way grandpa's cabin sits on a slight hill, and then your eye runs back and gets caught by the glimmer of the pond just before the wood line. Living here can truly be serene at times.

Finally making my way to the door of my barn, I open it and lay my keys on the table. Reaching for the light, I hear something fall off in the other corner. I took a step towards it and felt a white hot pain in the back of my head and crashed into the concrete floor. Half way regaining my consciousness, I rolled over and saw Blake standing over me, along with the center for our football team, Reggie White, who was holding a crow bar. I lift my head just off the concrete and start to say something, but the word is terminated by a diving right hand from Blake. I could feel my eye swelling, and blood trickling from my ear and mouth. He crouched over me, and holding my head up by my hair he said almost in a calm whisper, "Katie is mine you little rat, and she doesn't need you to protect her. If this ever happens again, you won't live to talk about it; do I make myself clear you fucking shit?" It must have been a rhetorical question, because without waiting for an answer he clocked me again.

My head bounced violently off the concrete. By this time, I was coughing up blood. Blake stood up to leave, but stopped suddenly, and then I saw him smile in the most menacing way I have ever seen a human being smile. He took a step towards me, planted that foot, and kicked my head with the other like he was going for the extra point. My vision was getting dimmer and the room had begun spinning. My heart was racing at some points but then it felt like it would completely stop for a few seconds. Then I hear the door slam open, shouts, and a horrifying female scream. The combination of shock and disgust made the scream so nasty, so blood curdling, it was worse than nails on a chalkboard. It was Katie, it had to be. The last thought I had was how good she looked today at Miller's, and then the world went black.

Love Bites

Waking up confused and with no idea what just happened isn't the easiest pill to swallow. Especially in an ambulance halfway to a hospital with your ex staring at you scared shitless. My ears were ringing from the cry of the sirens, and as fast as I'm sure we were going, everything was moving slow motion through my eyes—like watching my life through a slideshow. Katie was sitting beside me, holding my hand when I woke up.

"Oh my God Cole, you're awake! Are you okay?!"

"You're kind of squeezing the shit out of my hand but I think I'll live."

"Shut the fuck up! I was worried about you, for a minute I thought you might not make it." Through the vice grip on my hand, I could feel her trembling with fear.

"I'm glad you rode with me, I've missed holding your hand." She looked at me and half laughed in disbelief.

"Cole, you could've died today, and all you're worried about is the fact that I'm holding your hand? How bad did Blake fuck up that head of yours?"

"What can I say? I'm a hopeless romantic." As I said this, I tried lifting my head to view her response and the room once again began to twirl uncontrollably. She looked at me for a second, and then looked away, pulling her hand from mine. Fading in and out, a tear rolled down my cheek as I laid my head back on the gurney and let the darkness take over.

A brisk shake stirs me enough to open my eyes, and then intense pain and a smarting headache waken me abruptly. A doctor was at my side with his team of nurses. He greeted me with a smile and said, "Good Morning. My name is Dr. Stevenson and

I'm glad to see you with your eyes open for once; you gave your friends here a pretty good scare."

"Morning?" I asked confused.

"Yes. You were unconscious when you arrived here, and after treatment you remained stable but asleep throughout the night until now."

"Interesting. Oh and good morning too you doc. So do I get out of here today or what?"

"Well, you do have stitches in your lip, the back of your head, and just under your left brow, totaling thirty-six, and a minor concussion. Basically, you need to take it easy for a couple days, and maintain a diet of soft foods, and no driving until you complete a physical. All that said, I think it's reasonable to let you go right now, seeing as you can walk one end of the room and back for me." I nodded and let one of the nurses take out my IV. I then sat up slowly, edging to the side of the bed. The pain hit fast and hard, like a Mack truck to my head, so I sat there for a second putting my face in my hands.

The doctor looked at me and said, "Don't push yourself." What kind of advice is that? It infuriated me; like he thought I couldn't do it. I grabbed on to the arm of a chair and pulled myself off the edge of the hospital bed. I looked through the doctor to my goal, the wall. Taking my first step was shaky and confusing; it reminded me of going across an old rope bridge. I then took another, and another, and soon I was there. I turned around instantly and marched back towards the doctor, staring at him determinedly. Once I arrived, I looked him in the eyes, grinned, and then thought of something important…how am I going to get home?

"So there it is, doc. But I'm not so sure how I will get home since you won't let me drive."

"Well Mr. Harris, I was getting to that. You have a visitor this morning who has agreed to take you home, if that's okay with you."

"Sure, send them in."

"Okay. Well, you seem to be hell bent on getting better in a hurry so I'm sure you will be fine in no time. Just make sure you don't overdo it, and try to keep yourself out of trouble. Who even did this to you anyway?" I hesitated for a second as I tried to think of a viable story.

"I took a fall…a nasty one. Goddamn stairs right?"

"Yeah sure you did, kid. If you ever decide to file the report, which I would recommend by the way, the police will be on standby."

"No thanks, doc. Like I said, damn stairs." And with that, Dr. Stevenson walked out. Not ten seconds later there was a knock at the door.

Katie opened the door and walked in with some clothes and other necessities in hand. She looked overwhelmed with concern, but still found a way to smile when our eyes met.

"So I brought you your holey jeans you love so much, a thermal, your dirty blue flannel, and leather jacket. Is that okay?"

"Perfect, you know me too well. There's no way I'd be rocking the baggy sweat suit out of here."

"Yeah, I figured as much. Oh and I have your boots and deodorant too, because nobody wants to smell that hospital smell." I laughed and then began to get dressed. This was harder than I anticipated, and Katie had to help me a great deal. I could manage to pull my shirts over my head and pull my jeans on, but my boots proved to be too much. Katie helped me without hesitation, even though this was the first time we had been alone since she started dating Blake. She was just there for me, it was like we never skipped a beat together. We then made our way to the door to leave, but as I was about to open it, Katie looked at me and grabbed my hand as we walked out. At this moment, walking out of the hospital together hand in hand, I could not imagine myself any happier.

I realized how elated I was to be home when Katie pulled up next to my cabin in her Prius. I walked around to her side of the car for a second almost in a trance, just taking it in. Katie's arms around my waist surprised me, but then made it all that much sweeter. She lifted her head off of my shoulder, and whispered, "This place is beautiful, isn't it?"

"Yeah," I replied.

"I'm really glad you're okay." She put her head back on my shoulder, and then I felt a soft kiss on the back of my neck. Turning around as swiftly as I could, I smiled and then we stared deep into each other's eyes for what seemed like an eternity. Things were said during this time. Feelings were shared, sympathy, forgiveness, a bond strengthened by the mutual love being recognized without a single word uttered. Then, we kissed. It was smooth, it was gentle, and slow; it was absolute. I took a step back as she opened her door and with one last smile, she got in and began to drive away. For the first time in a long time, everything felt right again.

Well the honeymoon was over, and it had been for two weeks. Sixteen days to be exact. And that time will go by like two years when all you do is go to work, work out, and read the weekly news.

Physically, I was looking rough. A no calorie diet paired with drug use that would rival Keith Richards was taking its toll. The constant working out wasn't helping either.

Emotionally, I was unstable. It was partially because of the drugs, but mostly because, despite my efforts, Katie has chosen not to acknowledge me whatsoever since she took me home from the hospital.

Today won't be all bad, though. When I went into school for my online class, Tyler told me that he was going to come over after he and Elaine went out. Dinner and a movie I'm sure, that's cute. I'm surprised she is even letting him come over to be honest. I figured I would do a few odds and ends around the house and go get a quick workout in at Addison's gym while he's busy with her, it will clear my mind anyways.

Dismissal couldn't come quick enough today...or is that every day? In any event I arrived at my locker, and opening it to reveal my horror movie posters which included the original Texas Chainsaw Massacre, among others, putting at least a half smile on my face. That rapidly became a full-fledged smile when I saw the reaction of Kendra, a girl in my class who has had lockers next to me for as long as I can remember.

"Eww! Cole, why do you have to have those creepy things in your locker? It's gross."

"Awe Kendra, I love you too sugar. I'll tell ya what, you pick out a poster from wherever and I will hang it up in here just for you."

"I would appreciate that greatly," she said with a laugh. I felt a tap on my back as I was about to respond, and turning to look, I saw Blake. At first I thought he was going to hit me. Once I realized he wasn't going to, I wanted to hit him. I then thought about how everyone in the town knew he did what he did to me including my doctor, but he wouldn't receive community service for it even if I did report him doing it. He was like a god in this town. With all these emotions running through my head, there was only one thing I could say to him.

"You aren't going to make Reggie hit me with a crow bar again are you?"

"You really don't have to be a sarcastic asshole all the time, Cole. But then again that's vintage you isn't it?"

"Uh, sure...you really don't have to get hot and bothered all the time, Blake. Because I thought it was hilarious, but getting angry is kind of your thing right? BLAKE SMASH!!"

"Whatever. If we can be serious for a second, I wanted to say I was wrong for doing what I did. It meant a lot to Katie that you helped her even though she wants nothing to do with you, and maybe I overreacted. So yeah, sorry man." *Is this guy serious right now?*

"Well Blake, as moving as that was, and trust me, I will be pulling the puffs plus lotion out of my saddle bag in the parking lot, let's not waste each other's time here. We both know you aren't sorry and that you just want to rub it in that you still have Katie. Seriously did you think I would just hug you and say it was okay that you gave me thirty plus stitches? You can gag on it for all I care bud. I'm going to walk away now so I can get to the shit that I need to get done and you can go to practice and tackle sweaty guys in tights." Blake stood there, stunned as if Ali had just hit him with a stiff jab.

As I was walking out of school towards my bike, the little bit of good feeling that I had developed vanished instantaneously. Katie was there in front of me, walking from her last class to her locker with a couple of her friends. I stood there frozen, thinking back on the past few weeks. The missed calls, ignored texts, and the feelings of being an afterthought again. Everything was rushing back into my mind as I watched her walk past me. Her eyes met mine, and they pleaded with me to not acknowledge her. That, coupled with the muffled giggles of disapproval from her friends was enough to warrant silence, no matter how badly I wanted to talk to her. I walked out of school and headed home to stoke up my wood stove for the night.

While finishing the final split of the fallen oak into firewood, I paused and remembered that Tyler was supposed to swing by tonight. It was 10:30 p.m. already. I shook my head in disbelief and began to load the wheelbarrow. After stacking the final log and stoking the fire, I sat up convincing myself that there was a logical reason Tyler didn't show up tonight. It just wasn't like him to not say anything at all. Around two in the morning I convinced myself that I could just go in to school tomorrow and talk to him about it. I was sure he would have some crazy story to tell me and we would just laugh about it.

Addicted

The sweet sound of November Rain wakes me as I roll over to answer my cell phone. I leaned up on one arm and upon wiping my eyes read the name. It was Katie. Confused, I put the phone to my ear and answered, "Katie?"

"Cole! You have to get down to school right now! There's a big crowd and the cops are here, and they are saying things..."

"Katie, what's wrong?" She was in a panic, and it sounded like she was crying.

"Cole, they are saying things about Tyler. They, they are saying he's dead. Tyler is dead Cole." I was in so much shock I couldn't even respond, so I hung up the phone. I hurriedly got up and dressed; making my way outside and towards school. There's no way he's gone, no way. She's lying, she has to be lying.

I saw the massive crowd of high school kids standing outside the school as I came screeching into the parking lot. I hurriedly started walking towards them trying to push to the front.

"Hey, watch it!" yelled someone from behind me as I was frantically moving people out of the way. There wasn't time to look back or care about other people. This was life and death, and I needed to know about my best friend. When I finally got the front I saw the principal, Mr. Smith, standing there about to make his way inside to his office. As I started to move towards him, I was pulled back by my leather jacket.

"You can't talk to him right now Cole. I know you are upset but you have to let the principal do his job." It was Mrs. Jameson, one of my old math teachers. She was always a better counselor than a math teacher.

"I have to Mrs. J; I have to find out what happened to Ty!"

"Cole, listen to me, he doesn't have time for you right now, if you go into his office all it's going to do is get you in trouble and then you will never find out. You need to just wait for the police statement like everyone else. They are about to make their official statement, that's what everyone is here waiting on."

"Yeah, well I can't wait. That kid was like my brother. Just tell me where it happened and I'll leave."

"Cole, nobody is to have that information; you know that." Starting to become infuriated, I grabbed Mrs. Jameson, put her against the wall and in a cold tone stated that if she didn't tell me the location of Tyler's accident I would get to the principal, and "tear through" anyone who got in my way until I got answers. Mrs. Jameson is shaking violently underneath my grip. She's looking at me in fear, horrified of what's in front of her.

"The crime scene is back in the woods; just below the ridge line on the outskirts of the old town cemetery," she muttered. Letting go, I took the information and I started back towards my motorcycle. "Cole!" she exclaimed. Looking back, I listened for what she had to say. "If anyone finds out you are there, or that I told you, we are both toast." I just nodded. "Hey," she said as I was walking away, "Be careful, kid." With a half grin I turned and pulled out on my motorcycle headed towards the ridge as fast as two wheels could carry me.

I pulled into the cemetery and no sooner than I could shut off my Harley I was approached by an officer. "Sir, this is a closed crime scene and you have ten seconds to leave before I take you away in the patrol car." Looking through his arms as he was shying me away I could see a bunch of officers and a forensic team frantically working, and then I froze. There it was, on a gurney lay a big, heart breaking black body bag. I was stunned. I could feel the officer's hands trying to get me to turn around and leave but I couldn't move. Eventually he got forceful enough to snap me out of it, and I drove back home unable to believe what I just saw.

Once I parked the bike in the garage, I walked inside and sat there. I didn't know what to do. The one person who had always been there for me was gone. So I did what I usually do, I grabbed a bottle of whiskey and tried to numb the pain.

A fifth in and I'm still losing it. There was a hole growing in my heart so big and empty no amount of alcohol or recreational substance could fill it. Drink by drink, line by line, the hours pass while the pain persists. My phone has been going nuts with people trying to make sure I'm alright. There's nothing they can do to make it go away. How could they? What can you possibly say to make this alright? Tyler is dead. One of the only people I've loved in my life is gone and never coming back and for some reason I feel responsible. I have to find out what happened. I have to go back tonight.

As I was coming up on the cemetery, I noticed the patrol lights off behind it and pulled over. I thought about what Mrs. Jameson told me about not letting anyone see me headed towards the crime scene. Sitting there pondering a way to get around the fuzz, I remembered that the ridge has one main road to most people. To a kid who was always looking for cheap thrills, however; I knew there was an old dirt road used by the caretaker of the cemetery. It led straight back to an old pole barn and family mausoleum at the back end of the cemetery. I quietly drove past

the turn for the Old Eden Cemetery and began the long winding

ride up Ridge Road.

It was just before three a.m. when I hit the other side of

the ridge. Just before the bottom, I took a left onto an old dirt road

leading to the backside of the cemetery. Upon arriving, I shut off

the bike and rolled her inside the dark security of the mausoleum.

I grabbed my flashlight and knife and headed down through the

woods towards the back end of the cemetery.

As I slowly made my way to the scene, I saw no lights

or patrolmen on duty. They must have just posted guards at the

gate or something. In any event, I headed towards the caution tape

meticulously. As I approached, I began to soak in the brutality of

what had happened. No wander the town was keeping it so under

wraps. There was an unbelievable amount of blood on the ground.

I've never seen anything like it. There was a perfect circle drawn

in the ground around all the mess, which was weird to me. I knelt

down next to the gory scene and the tears began to flow. This

blood had to be Tyler's . All that was left of my friend was on the ground next to me. I've never cried harder in my life than in this moment.

Amidst my mourning, I heard a shift in the brush behind me. Instantly alerted, I went to check it out; making sure the police hadn't spotted me. Crouching low, I made my way towards the thick woods beside the cemetery. I heard faint noise continue beyond the wood line, and became intrigued. Suddenly, out of the corner of my eye, I saw something, someone, move swiftly into the darkness. *Was someone watching me?* Another dark mass just moved on the other side. Now I'm beginning to sweat. Reaching carefully for my knife I made my way over and began to trek through the dense woods. Staying low, knife in hand, I pursued. Listening, following a faint chant; too faint to make out still. Always staying alert for the mysterious shadows that had led me into the woods, I had made it at least a mile in. The chanting was loud now. It's a different language, I can't put my finger on it but I've heard it before. Then, up in the distance, I see a clearing. There's a fire. And around the fire people dressed in black chanting and dancing around a singular person in a dark robe.

Is this Real Life? I was astonished by just how many people were there. It had to be 20, maybe 30 people dancing around this guy. He was playing a pipe in the middle. Standing beside him was some sort of table, it was too far away to say for sure but I think there was a body on the table. I began to study the man leading them, watching his moves, trying to figure out what was happening. They continued to dance for a couple minutes, and then they all circled the table. The group of people waved their arms and danced along as the robed man chanted an incantation at the head of the table. He held his hands out over the lumpy mass on the table. The group pranced counter clockwise around him ecstatically.

I could feel the goose bumps popping up all over my body. *What was I watching?* Suddenly, the groups singing dulled down to a sinister, deep whisper. They continued their counter clockwise motion, moving swift and quiet. The robed man in the middle's chant became serious sounding. I strained to listen close, trying to make out the words in the chant, but to no avail. Then, the group around him began to move faster in their circle. Faster and faster they moved around him, until they were almost sprinting around this alter. Confused and terrified, I watched on awaiting a clue to what this was. All at once, the group slammed to the ground in unison, bowing their heads and joining hands as the robed man reached onto the table and grabbed part of what was on the table. He mumbled something slowly, and then let out a shriek as he lifted up what was in his hands. The group looked on with praise as he held it up for all of them to see. As he turned, the moonlight caught him and his treasure, and I couldn't believe what I was seeing. He was holding up Tyler's head! I tried to look away but it was like something was keeping me locked into this terrible scene. *Was this real? Was I dreaming?* The moon light was like a giant spotlight on the man. I could see every detail of the head he was holding. It was him. It was Ty. A burning sensation began taking over my body rapidly. I tried to look away once more and realized that the man holding Tyler's head was Glaring at me with fiery eyes.

I ran like I've never ran before. I stumbled hurriedly towards the mausoleum and mounted my bike, immediately leaving. I'm not sure that I touched the breaks the entire ride home, but what I do know is that once I got there I dove straight into the bottle again. My best friend was gone, and not in any accident or tragedy. He was brutally murdered—and I had to see him. The comfort coming through in the bitter oak flavor slowly glosses over the fact that I may be going insane.

Waking up nothing changed. I sat on the couch in shock. Were those people in the woods Tyler's killer? Was I entirely sure I actually saw anything? My mind was racing with possibilities, doubt, and a touch of paranoia. Should I tell someone? Would anyone even believe me?

I left the house after a drink, heading towards school. It was Wednesday, so I would have to wait for Katie to get out of school before I could talk to her about all of this unless I wanted a one way ticket to the nut house; so I waited.

The clock finally hit 3:20 and the rush of students began. A sea of kids takes over the sidewalks and everyone blends in, everyone but Katie. I could pick her out of a crowd of a thousand. She was fresh out of the doors, walking with a few of her friends; laughing about something or another. Her long curls lay perfectly and its fawn color accentuates her blue eyes making them that much more piercing.

"Jesus!" She yells suddenly. Her heart races until she notices my ring, and then she turns slowly. "Cole, you scared the shit out of me. I thought I was getting kidnapped or something."

"Yeah I bet, right up until you saw this right?" I flash my ring to her. It is just a simple sterling silver band with beveled edges, but she would recognize it anywhere. She got it for me for my last birthday, and it has our initials on the underside—*CH&KH forever*. She said it was meant to be because we already had the same last initial.

"Yeah, until I knew it was you. What are you doing here anyway? I figured you would stay as far away as possible from this place after what happened to Tyler." That was the first time I heard his name out loud since he died. It was the first time that someone mentioned him dying to me, and it hit like a freight train. I was silent as a tear ran down my left cheek.

"Cole, I'm really sorry." She started. "I didn't mean to upset you."

"It's okay," I muttered as I grabbed her hand and said, "I came here to get you so I could talk to you about it."

"Okay then, let's go."

I took her back to my house and sat her down in the living room, trying to think of how to start this conversation. I mean how is she supposed to believe all this? I wasn't so sure I believed it myself.

"So I know this must be tearing you up inside. What did you do all night after you found out? I know you weren't too stable when you got the news at school." She was right. I wasn't stable at all. I could tell she was concerned about the way I acted yesterday, and she should be given she knows my history with recreational drugs.

"Yeah it is. And no, I wasn't stable; I'm still not. I went to the cemetery last night. I found out the scene was there and I took a back road in behind the mausoleum." I could see the look on her face. That look of concern you get when you realize that the person you're talking to is crazy.

"Cole, why did you do that?! Don't you realize that is illegal?"

"Yeah I do, but I had to see him. My only friend was dead Katie, don't try to act like you know what that feels like because you don't. Anyways, the reason I wanted to talk to you was because I saw something when I was there. Something awful." She was crying until this point. She looked up in shock at my last words.

"What is it?" I was silent. Remembering everything that I saw was bad enough, but hearing it out loud might drive me insane. "What did you see Cole?!" My mind was racing. I was trying so hard to remember everything I saw. It was mixing together and going a hundred miles per hour. The combination of the death of my friend, sneaking out to see the scene, and everything I thought I had seen was weighing too heavy on me. Throw all the pills and the alcohol on top of that and I couldn't make sense of anything. I did my best with it, however; and I cleared my throat to begin to tell her.

"I…I saw the murder scene. I saw my best friend's blood stained into the grass." I had to stop so I could wipe the tears from my eyes. Katie was so upset she was shaking.

"I'm so sorry Cole" she sobbed, "I had no idea. They aren't saying anything about it in town." She moved close and gave me a tight hug. I spent a minute lost in her arms. It felt so right having her there. But I had to tell her more. I pushed her back and stared as I tried to put the words together.

"Katie, that wasn't all that I saw. There was more." She looked at me, perplexed.

"What do you mean?"

"Well, when I was in the cemetery, I heard something behind me. I thought maybe the police had heard me crying or something so I looked but nothing was there. And then I saw someone run past me through the woods." Katie was listening intently but I could tell she was wondering where I was going with this. I continued again quietly, saying "I followed it into the wood line behind the cemetery. Walking quietly, I listened for anything moving beside me. The deeper in I got, the more rustling and laughing I could hear around me but I couldn't see anyone. Knife in hand I walked until I saw a clearing up ahead. There were people dancing and chanting around a fire. And there was a man in the middle in a dark robe. He was playing a flute and there was a table with a book and something else on it. And while I was watching them, the man lifted up..he lifted up Tyler's head. I thought I was going to puke. The man saw me watching and he stared at me like I was a dead man. I ran after that and drove home." Katie was staring at me in silence. She was absolutely stunned by what I was saying, and I could tell she didn't believe it. "I think they were a cult or something Katie."

"Cole, are you sure that happened? I mean after everything you've been through, maybe your mind was tricking you. You could've even had a nightmare last night you never know. I think you just need to rest. Everything is driving you crazy you know?" I knew she wouldn't believe that I saw that.

It's easy to write it off as the stress from losing your best friend, and believe me I wanted to do the same thing—but this was real.

"I figured you would say that, and just so you know, it wasn't a nightmare because I didn't sleep last night. How could I?" Something about her just brushing it off made me furious. "What if I went back? What if I could prove it to you?"

"No, Cole. You aren't going back there. For one, it's a crime scene and that's illegal, and second; don't you think it messed you up enough the first time? I mean you're talking about seeing people in the woods and not making any sense. And I see you've been drinking a little too." She was holding up two empty bottles of whiskey. I can't believe she is brushing this off as if I'm just some junkie.

"So what then, I'm just making it up because I'm grieving? I wouldn't do that Katie. I thought maybe you would believe me because you know how I am."

"Yes I do know how you are. That's part of the reason I don't believe you."

"What do you mean that's part of the reason?"

"You know what I mean Cole. Don't make me say it."
I was livid now. I can't believe she was doing this to me.

"No, I want you to say it. Go ahead Katie. Be
judgmental like everyone else."

"You're an addict Cole. And I don't know if you will
ever stop. Any time you have a problem you dive farther and
farther in and it just gets worse. You are on a path to self-
destruction and it's pathetic. I'm sorry I have to tell you but it's
true." I couldn't even say anything to that. I stood there, furious.
She moved closer and started to say something again.

"I know you've been through a lot, but you need help."
I stopped her right there as I angrily put my fist through the wall
ending her get help speech.

I pulled it back out and stared. As the blood trickled
and drywall fell to the ground I looked up and said, "Walk away
from me."

Part of me couldn't believe Katie of all people just said
those words to me. "You're an addict." Another part of me,
however; was starting to agree. Everyone in town already thought

it, and had for months. Now the only person who ever had faith that I wasn't just said to my face that I was. On top of that, I really was losing it over Tyler. I was sure that what I told Katie about seeing him and the cult was true, but I know for a fact that they wrapped up the crime scene before I ever got there. The memory was so vivid though. The macabre feel of it, the sights, and even the smells; I remembered it all as if it had happened. But if I wasn't sure that had happened, then what I thought I saw in the woods surely had to be a hallucination. With a million thoughts swirling in my head, I made it through another long, sleepless night with the help of a little Jonny Walker.

The Truth about Eden

For the past two days I've sat silent at the house, all the while losing control on the inside. I haven't slept, ate, or drank anything besides alcohol. I haven't spoken an actual word out loud since speaking with Katie. With Eden being a small town it's inevitable that word about me being at the cemetery would get out, and with that the rumors would start.

People were looking at me like I was a freak. Not that they didn't before, but this is different. They made me feel like Charles Manson or something. None of that matters though, because after I heard the cause of death of Tyler this morning, I can only think about what I really did see that night in the woods.

"The suicide of eighteen year old Columbia High student Tyler Moore is not only tragic for his family and friends, but for our community." Those were the words I heard on the press conference held by the police department this morning. They were seriously saying it was a suicide? I saw Tyler; I saw his pool of blood and it looked like he was cut open and drained by several people. Speaking of several people, I saw a group of freaks dancing around while a man in a robe held up Tyler's decapitated head for Christ's fucking sakes. Either I was officially insane or the town was hiding something. Whatever the case, I had to go back and get some answers.

As I took the last swig of Jameson, I put out my cigarette and headed off towards the cemetery. It's a cold dreary night and I have no idea what I'm about to ride into. But I was determined. There was something more to Tyler's death, I could feel it.

The fog rolled thick and ankle high as I made my way through the graves to the wood line on the backside of the cemetery. An assortment of sounds began to hit my ears once entering the woods. The intense sounds of the outdoors at night tend to make your mind race or even play tricks on it, but not tonight. I'm focused. I'm focused on finding out what happened to my best friend, and nothing was going to stand in the way of me and the truth.

As I was getting closer to the same clearing I saw before, I could hear the town bells chime. It was midnight. Then in the distance, I could hear it. There is a soft chanting sound coming from just ahead, but that wasn't all. I could hear faint laughter coming from just out of my eyesight. Not the innocent kind of laughter, and not the sound of wind or something I could be mistaking for a laugh, but an evil kind of cackle coming from the darkness.

I was close, closer than the first time. Hiding behind the bush, I could see a large fire and people. Not just standing, but sitting in rows of four. There were twelve all together, seated almost like a congregation. And standing in front of them is a man reciting something from behind a table. I fix my attention on this man. The table was cloaked in animal furs, and there is a set of three candles at either end. In the middle there is cups, or chalices, and a few other things I can't make out. The chanting is getting louder. It isn't a language I have ever heard before. The people were beginning to get up now. The man leading the procession picked up a pipe and began to play a song. The song is eerie, but captivating. His people began to follow him. They were dancing now. They left, proceeding deep into the woods single file, behind the man with the flute. I sat there for a few minutes wondering what exactly I just witnessed. *What were they doing out here?* It was almost like a mass. Like one of those backwoods crazy groups you read about in books. I had to know everything about these people and what they were doing out here. I was headed for the library first thing come daylight.

Eden's town library is a beautiful gothic style building, and huge too; despite its lack of use. Its enormous pointed arches and ornate stone work strike you from the moment you walk through the double oak doors. The entire structure is limestone, and the building bears a remarkable resemblance to an old time castle down to the six gargoyle statues mounted on its face. The Ribbed vaults allow for many high windows and massively high and elegant ceilings. This gives the hall leading to the main desk an eerie, almost vampiric feel. I always felt it was the most beautiful and scary thing that I had ever seen growing up here. Every detail is beautiful; seeing the stained glass windows, the huge center piece rugs, hand carved chairs and desks, and just sitting in one of the circle rooms almost makes you feel as if you belong in one of the Grimm brothers fables.

I made my way to the main desk, hoping the lady could help direct me to what I was looking for. Mrs. Pearl Winifred was a nice enough lady not to deem me crazy when I asked about the section on the Occult, so I went to her for assistance. She is a staple of the town and has been working the front desk in the Eden library since I can recall. "Down the stairs to the left hand side," was her response to a question I'm sure she doesn't hear too often.

I made my way down the stairwell, which was old and tightly quartered, and in the third row to the left, I found my section. There were various books on demonology as a study, and theological books about Satan and the devil. And of course a few books on famous folktales such as *The Devil and Tom Walker* and legends of real life people including, the 27 club, for example.

Being a rock and roll fan, I remembered reading about the story behind the 27 club in high school. Since Robert Johnson started singing songs like *Crossroads,* and *Hell Hound on my Trail*, there were rumors of a deal with the devil. Johnson was the first rumored to sell his soul for the ability to play guitar, but a rash of extremely talented musicians dying at his same age of 27, a prevalent belief started in the musical society that these deals were real. I always laughed at the idea, and considered it more of a conspiracy theory that rivaled aliens and Bigfoot. Not quite knowing where to start or what exactly I was looking for, I reached for one of the books on demonology. Just as my hand touched the binding, I could feel someone move swiftly up behind me and put their hand on mine stopping me. Taken off guard, I pulled my hand away and turned around to see a man staring back at me coldly.

"Excuse me," I started, "if you need this book or something it's yours man." He was an older man, around fifty maybe, and looked worn. His clothes were dirty and tattered. He was an intimidating man, tall in nature, and his shoulder length hair and beard gave off an unkempt and off-putting vibe.

"That's not it, son." I was confused now. He had a peculiar look on his face and I really couldn't tell if he was going to say something else or jump me right there in the library. "I'm here to help you," he continued, "I'm here to tell you that the answers to your questions aren't in any book. Or at least not in the books at this library."

"I'm sorry mister, but I have no idea what you're talking about." Who was this guy? I certainly had never seen him before, and there was no way he could *actually* know why I was here.

"Don't play dumb with me kid. We both know you've done some snooping in the woods. And you don't know what you're getting into, and you're lucky you haven't gotten your fool self killed."

"Who are you?" I was perplexed to say the least. This guy knew I was in the woods, which means he knows what I saw. How was that even possible?

"I'm somebody who knows a little something about something. I'm somebody who's been where you're at now, and most importantly, I'm someone who can help."

"What do you mean *help?*"

"Well first of all, we've got to get you to a real library. If you follow me back to my place I can show you everything you need to know."

"I don't know. I don't even know who you are or how you know about anything."

"I know you don't think you can trust me, but I am on your side here. You're on the right path so far kid, and by that I mean what you saw does have something to do with your friend, Tyler. I can help you if you let me. It won't be easy, and a lot of it is going to sound crazy, but if you can meet me at town's edge tonight, I can open your eyes." Hearing him mention Tyler almost did me in. I couldn't believe he knew about him. And he was saying that something bad really *did* happen to him. I felt crazy for even considering trusting a total stranger from God knows where, but I had to know what happened to Tyler.

"Did you find everything okay young man?" Mrs. Winifred's high pitched voice invaded our conversation and my thoughts. She had thrust herself between the two of us, putting her hands on either of our shoulders. She was staring at me intently, and had quite a grip on my arm.

"Yeah, yeah I'm okay Mrs. Winifred. Thank you for your help." She smiled a fake kind of smile as I practically had to rip her hand from me to leave. I made eye contact with the man over her and he nodded. I looked away, uncertain. I needed to go back home. I needed time to clear my head and decide if I could actually go through with this or not. With a troubled mind and heavy heart, I got on my bike and started the drive back to the cabin.

As I turned down my road, I could hear what sounded like several sirens and there was smoke rising from somewhere. This was nothing new, houses on this road where old and electrical shorts were no surprise. Once I got about halfway down the road, however; I could see flames shooting high. It was grandpas. I just knew it was. I flew towards the cabin only to confirm my fears. I pulled in the driveway behind two fire trucks and three patrol cars. Locking the brakes of my bike, I threw it to the side as fast as I could and ran towards the house screaming. I made it about forty or fifty feet before an officer tackled me to the ground, shortly followed by two more to make sure I stayed contained. The heat coming from the fire was immense, more so than anything I have ever experienced. As an hour passes, I sit in a patrol car, handcuffed at a safe distance as they try to fight the fire. I could not believe it. I watched them try for another thirty minutes, but there was nothing they could do. Everything was gone. The house and garage were now down to their foundations. As the presiding officer tried to console me, my mind faded out and I broke down. I began to cry harder than I ever remembered crying. I had lost everything that mattered to me. I had nothing left. Nothing but a long haired stranger from the library. I collected myself, told the officers that I had a place to stay until things were figured out, and got on my bike; headed for the edge of town.

As soon as I hit the bridge heading out of town, I could see an old car parked in the pull off. I slowed down and pulled in, parking my bike. Nobody was moving from the vehicle. It was an old Camaro,'79 or '80 with the Z28 package. Whoever did own this car, I admired their style. Then suddenly the lights flashed and the car pulled away heading out of town.

Starting my motorcycle furiously, I tried to keep up as we flew through the twists and turns of back roads I had never seen before. The farther we went, the more lost I became. The road became more and more narrow, and the traffic was nonexistent. The tree branches from either side came together over the road in a perfectly eerie sense causing extreme darkness. We were starting to slow now. Almost instantaneously the Camaro slams his breaks and takes a left onto a dirt road. I skidded and swerved, nearly laying over my hardtail. About a hundred yards up, we turned right onto another dirt pathway. This time you could see an old plantation home ahead.

Three stories with a wraparound porch and mahogany door with stained glass inserts. The house itself was dirty and rotting, like something straight out of a classic haunted house story. The Camaro stopped and parked to the side of the driveway.

I slowed and put my feet down keeping my distance. Sure enough out stepped the man from the library.

"Glad you could keep up through the turns on your pony Cinderella." We both laughed, but before I could respond, he looked at me intently and continued, "You did the right thing coming here tonight, but nothing about what I'm about to tell you is going to be easy or even make sense. Tonight I'm going to open your eyes to the truth about the peaceful little town of Eden."

"I risked my bacon following your crazy ass out here didn't I?" I responded without hesitation. "I want to know everything that you know. Tell me about these people. Tell me why I've lost everything."

"That's what I like to hear," he said while motioning me towards the house. "Welcome to the Wright family manor. Name's John by the way. This thing has been in my family since the slave days, and you're welcome to stay as long as you keep that open mind frame you have now."

As run down as the outside appeared, the inside is very elegant; although cluttered. Taking time to look through the dust, you could find amazing detail in every corner of this century old home. Hand carved wood trim is placed generously around the house, along with hand carved railings and tin ceilings. I felt like I was walking through a time machine. We turned a corner out of the foyer, passing through the formal dining room and through a pocket door, arriving at the study. This was a massive room, with a massive amount of books, too. My eyes were dancing from shelf to shelf, each filled with dust-covered hardbacks.

"Sit down here," John ordered as he pointed to an old desk. I pulled out the leather upholstered chair and sat down. "Now the first thing you need to know is this library is key. Without it, you will never hold the knowledge necessary to be any use to me."

"Yes sir," I mutter sarcastically. John then threw a book down in front of me. I wiped the dust off of the front of the book, uncovering the title, which read: The Gospel of the Witches.

"Witches?" I asked, stunned. "This is no time for fairytales, pal."

"It's no time to be a smartass, either. What you saw out there, son, was an offering. A mass if you will. This book is a translation done from the original texts. The Gospel will set you in the right direction as far as who the witches worship and why they do it. It does come up short on a few things, though. Basically, the guys from Salem weren't all that crazy. Just let me know when you're done with this one and I will give you the next text book." I don't know what to think. Witches? I thought they were just a product of hysteria and old hags from Disney stories. I do know what I saw out there; however. And if this explains it, then so be it.

I began to read and made it swiftly through the story of the beginning. It was the story of a goddess named Diana giving birth to a daughter, Aradia. The story goes as follows:

Diana greatly loved her brother, Lucifer, god of the Sun and of the Moon, the god of Light, who was so proud of his beauty, and who for his pride was driven from Paradise. Diana had by her brother a daughter, whom they named Aradia.

John said to ignore the details of the gospel, because it was *their* gospel. By this meaning they worship these creatures, so their gospel overlooks certain things and spins what happened in a positive way. Basically the book went on to say that Diana had taken the form of Lucifer's favorite cat, thus tricking him into fathering their daughter, Aradia. Diana was the goddess of darkness, so in this sense, darkness had conquered light. Diana then sent her daughter to be reborn on earth as a mortal to teach witchcraft to the poor who lived in the woods as thieves and assassins. They were to use this knowledge to overthrow the rich who they refer to as "the evil race."

I looked at John, intrigued by what I had just read.

"You wanna explain to me what this all means?" I asked, overwhelmed.

"Sure. As far as a Diana or Aradia goes, I have never heard of any hard proof of witches worshiping them. But what we do know is that Lucifer was cast from Paradise for his pride, you've heard the story from the bible of course. It's also accurate in some ways.

Lucifer was an archangel, and obsessed with his own beauty, he refused to bow to human kind and was cast to hell."

"I remember the story in the Bible from when I was little. How does that tie into what I saw in the woods?"

"Well, what you need to know is that witches are no good Satanists who will no sooner kill you than blink." I'm in disbelief listening to John go on about something I laughed at until tonight. Now we were talking life and death.

"The best I can tell," John continued, "Is that the witches wrote in Aradia as a mockery of Jesus of Nazareth. You will often find that anything to do with the demonic is meant to in some way diminish God, the trinity, or the Christ child. Now as far as Diana, it is believed that is a code name for Lilith."

"Lilith? Who is that?" My mind is swirling with all this information and it just keeps coming.

"Lilith is Lucifer's first. She's sometimes referred to as his mate or wife, or the queen of all monsters. In a biblical sense, she was the first failed wife of Adam."

"Adam, like naked in a garden craving an apple Adam?" I knew I was interrupting often but this was just too much to take in. My life was turning into an epic of the old days.

"Yeah that's the one." John smiled a kind of half smile, and while patting me on the back continued, "You'll learn fast that everything is actually backwards in life. The fairytales we read as kids were never meant to be forgotten, Cole." I'm not even sure what to think at this point. In such a short time my entire world has been flipped upside down. My friend is dead, my grandpa's cabin is in ruins, and I'm in a stranger's library talking about fairytales being real. At any rate I decided to shut my trap and listen.

"God made Lilith at the same time as Adam," John started again, "She was meant to be his female companion. But feeling equal to Adam, she refused to submit sexually to him; she only wanted to be in a top dominant position. She then fled. Once found by the angels, she was given the choice to go back but instead chose to be the mother of all demons. The Old Testament picks it up slightly after this, when trying to cure Adam's loneliness; God creates Eve from the rib bone of Adam leading to the story in the Garden."

John decided that was enough for the night, and after talking over a few glasses of Johnny Walker, he sent me up to the third floor attic. When John inherited this property, he finished the attic into a private guest suite. "It hasn't been used in a while," he stated, "But make yourself at home."

I made my way up the dark stained walnut master staircase; running my hand along the smooth, intricate details of the rails. I arrived on the third floor, and turned a corner down a short hall leading to my room. As I opened the massive door, I began to take it all in. The old hickory floors, English oak wood trim, and rod iron bed. This room was the most beautiful room I had ever seen. While it was beautiful, it was however; rather empty. There was a big mahogany dresser in the corner as you walked in, a nightstand on either side of the aforementioned bed, and a chair in the end corner just beside the picture window at the end of the room. Sitting on the edge of the bed, I just started reflecting on everything. For the first time since I drove up on that fire, the sadness was sinking in. John's words weren't helping.

This room wasn't helping. 'Make yourself at home.' I couldn't

stop thinking about that. This wasn't home. My home was ash on

the damp autumn ground. How am I supposed to make myself at

home when I don't even have clothes to fill the damn dresser in the

corner? I began to undress for bed, trying to ease my mind. I

threw the only clothes I had to my name onto the rocking chair,

and opened the covers. I kissed my grandfather's dog tags and

removed the sterling silver ring Katie gave me last year. Wiping a

tear from my eye, I shut the lamplight off and rolled over to sleep.

The Art of Self Preservation

I woke up realizing I had a big plate full of problems to begin dealing with. I couldn't just ignore the fact that my house had burnt down. There were many things needing to be tied up with that. There were all kinds of insurance questions going around, and of course they wanted an investigation to see how the fire started in the first place. I needed to start sorting that out today. On top of that, I hadn't been to work since the Friday before I found out about Tyler.

I got dressed and headed downstairs looking for John. I found him in the study, with a book open and coffee cup in hand.

"Well good morning, princess." He said as he looked up from his mug. He stopped after saying that for a second, and then laughed. "You gonna take a shower son or are you just gonna walk around smelling like a rock star all day?"

"I wasn't sure if there was a shower in this two hundred year old hunk old man." I had to fire back with something witty. I usually don't get comfortable enough to do that with anyone except my close friends, but something about John made me feel like I had known him forever. He felt like family.

"Sure does, kid. You've even got your own on the attic room floor. Take the stairs to the third floor and go left instead of right. That part of the hallway dead ends into the bathroom door. I think it'll suit your needs."

I nodded and made my way up the stairs to the third floor. I walked the short hall to another beautifully ornate, and massive, wooden door. Walking into this bathroom was like walking into another house. The sheer size of it was utterly impressive.

The ivory colored floor tiles caught my eye immediately. The double vanity was an antique dresser or some old piece of furniture that had been white washed and had matching porcelain sinks. Across the room diagonally from the double vanity was a matching white washed armoire that was being used to hold all the linens and bathroom supplies. Just next to the armoire was a beautiful white claw bath tub. The legs on this antique piece were made of beautiful polished nickel to match the shower head attached at one end.

Just behind the tub was an immaculate floor to ceiling glass tile window. The amount of natural light coming in deemed no man made lights necessary. I finally looked up to see the shower at the end of the room. It is a stone walk in shower, with a curved stone wall enclosing the shower from the rest of the room. The earth tone colors of the stone gave it such a relaxing feel.

I undressed and walked through the open entrance to the shower. Straight ahead on the far wall was a hand shower with massaging heads that you could turn on and use, but I chose to turn on the rain style shower head directly above. On either side of me there was three body spraying heads that came on. This shower is the most relaxed I can remember being in a long, long time.

After about an hour passes, I finally got dressed and made my way downstairs. I grabbed my leather jacket off the coat rack in the foyer, and met John on my way outside. I explained to him that I had some things to take care of with my place, and he answered with a simple nod to let me be on my way.

It took about a whole five minutes to get thrown back on my ass in Alwen's parking lot once arriving to town. Apparently managers aren't allowed to not show up to work for a week. I expected as much, honestly. I picked myself up and rode my Harley over to grandpas. I was supposed to meet the insurance agent there to talk about numbers and my plans with the property.

I arrived at the house to see Kevin Walker, Elaine's Uncle, waiting by his car. Kevin was an insurance salesman and part time real estate agent here in Eden, and was well known amongst the town people. He is the kind of man that you love or you hate. I walked up to Kevin and greeted him with a handshake.

"How are ya, Cole?!" He said with convincing enthusiasm. "How's Katie doing these days?" Kevin was the first person to make that mistake since Katie and I had parted ways six months ago. No fault of his, of course, but now the memories were flooding in like a title wave. All the memories spent in my truck talking the night away, or looking up at the stars in the middle of a hot summer night, all the wonderful times that I was lucky enough to be hers were hitting me with the full force of a semi-truck. I stood there blank and unassuming, reflecting on her for what must have been a long enough time to make Kevin realize something was up. I looked up to catch his eye, and it was painfully obvious that he had stuck his own foot in his mouth, so I quickly changed subject for him.

"I'm doing okay all things considered, how about you Mr. Walker? And I hope Elaine is doing well after Ty. What's your plan of action with grandpa's property if I can ask?" Now Kevin Walker was always a little off with people, but I noticed something odd while we were talking. He had a halfcocked smile, which began with the mention of Elaine. It was almost like he was smirking. He quickly followed his awkward smile with a hand gesture leading me up the drive toward the place where my grandfather's cabin used to sit.

"Well for starters, I'll give you the rundown on what the police and fireman's report found. There was no sign of an electrical short, and no sign that this was a case of arson. So basically your name has been cleared for sure and the insurance check will be coming to you shortly for the value of the cabin."

"How much exactly would that be, Mr. Walker?" I felt like I had to ask. Money was the last thing on my mind right now. I was lost in the fact that the house I was raised in was gone forever. A place I loved and took care of just vanished. Kind of like everything else in my life at this point actually, but we are here on the business of insurance, so I had to ask.

"Well Cole, your grandfather had this house insured sometime before he died with a policy of 359,000 dollars. That's a handsome amount for this town, and surely enough to rebuild a cabin similar to your grandfathers, but my suggestion to you would be to sell this land Cole." Typical response from Kevin. He has been hounding me and my grandfather before me to sell the land ever since he got wind of it. Our land is well known as a fine place for hunting and fishing, and is heavily wooded, providing plenty of privacy.

"I'm not selling my grandpa's land, Kevin, so you can get it out of your little head okay?" My response was harsh, but so were the circumstances. I was here standing in front of a few boards still standing on what used to be the foundation to a beautiful hand built red cedar cabin given to me by my grandfather after it has just burnt to the ground and this asshole is only thinking about an investment opportunity for himself. Kevin started to say something or another, but I just turned and walked away. I wanted to walk through what was left of the house.

As I made my way up towards the house, I saw the ashy remains of my garage and remembered that it too had been burned to a crisp. My truck was in there. That beautiful, big diesel powered ford, gone. I clinched my fists and headed towards the house. I followed the drive and walked over where the door would have been. As I began to walk through and recreate the layout of the rooms in my mind, the memories made in those rooms started to take me over. All the times I ran like crazy through each one as a kid, the times I spent fixing and decorating them with my grandfather, and the time I had spent later making it my own. I stood in the middle dumbfounded. Somewhere behind me I heard Kevin making his way over the rubble.

"Cole, I understand that you're upset, and I am going to leave you be, I just thought you might want to hang on to some of this." Turning towards him to look, my eyes landed on a box. He explained that it was all the first responders could save from the house and garage. He handed me the box and promptly left me to myself.

There were only a few sparse items inside the tattered cardboard box; three pictures and what was left of my hickory wood splitting maul. I picked up the maul, examining its splintered and seared ends, and moved it aside to get to the pictures. The first one that I turned over was a picture of my grandfather. It was an old polaroid taken of him during his service in Korea. The withered edges and smoke damage distorted his image greatly, but it was beautiful to me. Next to it in the box was a picture of my mother holding me as a baby. I always kept this picture inside my console in the truck for good luck. She was my angel. Now all that was left of my picture of her was one corner, she was ripped and burnt from the collar bone down, and I was no longer present in the picture. I wiped my eyes and set it aside to grab the final picture. It was an 8x10 of Katie and I. We had our pictures professionally done at the end of last year together, and it was the happiest time of my life. studying the photo I could hear the laughter, see her smile, and feel the intense cold as we sat across the railroad tracks posing for the camera. My smile quickly faded as I realized this was just a memory, just like everything else had become.

I loaded the pictures and maul into the leather pack on my Harley and sped off back towards John's home.

I arrived and found John waiting on me in the foyer with his bottle of Johnny Walker and two glasses. He had a sincere look of worry and care on his face as he looked at me and asked, "What did you find out, kid?"

"What I found was a bunch of old memories and an old wood mauler, and the last thing that meant anything to me gone forever," I answered as I grabbed the glass and bottle pouring myself a drink. I walked past him to the dining room table and plopped down, hammering down the first round. "You know, a billion thoughts crossed my mind on the way over here," I continued as I poured another glass, "I thought back on all the memories made and all that I have lost in the past few days, and I thought about just wrapping my Harley around a tree and finishing the job." John looked up from his cup, frightened. "Then," I continued, "I realized a small detail I had overlooked on one of the pictures I found when I went to the cabin. The last picture I had found was of Katie and me. I was so messed up from the whole situation that it didn't even register that I was holding an 8x10 in my hands. Not only was it a big ass picture, but it was in immaculate condition, no smoke damage or burns. Then I remembered that I had that fucking picture framed and it was in my basement in a box buried somewhere."

"Well, that's some good work kid, really good fucking work," John replied as he caught on to my point. He sipped his drink and nodded for me to conclude, so I took one big drink finishing my whiskey off, stood up and started to do just that.

"So when I got here, I stopped and examined the picture again just to see what I missed, and I found this shit." I grabbed the picture out of my back pocket, unfolded it and slammed it onto the table. The back of this picture had a small symbol drawn in the left hand bottom corner. It consisted of two shapes, one a dark circle, and over top of that a crescent moon shape also filled in dark. John examined the symbol as I had shown it to him, and looked unsurprised by it all. He then looked to me, almost with a sense of excitement that I had stumbled onto something of this nature.

"I want to show you something, Cole." I leaned in to find out what it was I had discovered. "This symbol is no accident or random doodle as I am sure you have already guessed. The crescent shape over the circle here is indicative of the male *god*. It is the symbol of the horns. Now, most of these modern day wiccas or whatever they identify as, will do their best to convince you that these symbols are not satanic and that witches are good and wholesome and have nothing to do with the devil. But those people son, they are new age hippies who have no idea of the deities they are praying to." I was shocked to hear this. Witches are real and I had found proof of them in my town; burning down *my house*. And not the trendy, hot, *Charmed* style witch that I was used to either, he was talking evil hag, burn 'em at the stake, Satan loving witches. "Most always the horns will be intended to take the shape of a goats," John continued, "So anytime you run across goats, horns, or anything related to that, you know it isn't a coincidence."

This was happening for real. My mind was still racing. A simple photo given to me as a tool to mourn has shined light on who may have been behind this fire. Was it the people from the woods? Honestly, everything is pointing in that direction so far, whether I want to admit it or not. This raises an even stickier question as my mind continues to ponder; if it was them, then they know about me in detail and do not like that I was there. So then, what will be their next action?

John saw the intense look of curiosity coupled with anger on my face and must have tapped into it himself. He grabbed my shoulder with serious undertones and stated fiercely that we had 'work to do.' I stepped away from his grasp and back to my box of contents. Standing there collecting myself, I reached into the box pulling out the maul head and looked up with fire in my eyes. "The only things I have left from my life as I knew it are memories besides what is in this box, man. But as big as the hole in my heart is and as much as it hurts, I know I'm not alone now. So do you know what I'm going to do?" John's eyebrow raised with anticipation as a smirk appeared on his face as well. "I am going to take this wood mauler, make it new again, hunt down the son of a bitch who is responsible for tearing me apart, and I am going to bury it into their fucking chest plate. You in?"

John was full on smiling now. "You know I can get behind that, kid. I will teach you everything you need to know so we can hunt these bastards down and end them." A feeling of determination and trust was overwhelming me now. I felt like I had known John my entire life for some reason. I wanted so badly to know what he knew, and to kill anything that got in the way of me finding out who these *witches* were. John's smirk then dissipated as he turned to me once more. "I just want you to know, starting out this whole learning thing is going to suck for you. Lot of black eyes and headaches, but soon enough you will be ready. I'm sorry about everything you have been through Cole, I really am. But what doesn't kill you will make you stronger, kid. You just gotta trust me and hang in on this wild ride." Johns words meant a lot to me. This was the first time in a long time that someone had actually sympathized with me. He was wrong about one thing, however. I wasn't going to be ready 'soon enough,' I was ready now.

The Art of Self Preservation Part II

I was learning quickly what that whole "black eyes"
line meant when John said he would teach me all I needed to
know. The next morning after I brought the picture to his house, I
was taken out to the back garden to be shown "combat skills."
Strike quick and do as much damage as possible that was John's
big message. I remember looking at him like he was a fool when
he wanted to teach *me* combat moves. When I started high school
as a freshman, I got into lifting weights. I soon found out that
many of my friends I lifted with were boxing or doing some type
of martial arts to stay in shape. I began to enquire about getting
taught on the heavy bag at our local gym, and ended up having an
amateur career that lasted from then until the start of my senior
year. Needless to say I was arrogant from the get go when John
started in on his combat lessons. I have spent the past few weeks

getting the arrogance punched, grabbed, kicked, choked, and hip tossed right out of me. John still has not told me where he learned to do all of this, but he treats it as an art, and I've learned a lot these past few weeks.

First of all, fighting isn't about how many times you can punch someone, or footwork or how good your left cross is. At least it isn't in the real world. Fighting all comes down to anticipation of the other person's body, quick reactions to their movements, and pinpoint striking to specific areas of the body. I learned to punch once to the body, let the person lean forward instinctively and plan my next shot from there as opposed to throwing multiple shots to the body. Also, John taught me to aim for elbows, collar bones, knees, the sternum, and the throat. These are very sensitive spots of the body that most people do not expect to be hit in. It has taken me a while to get it all down, but lately, the student has been becoming the sensei if you catch my drift. More focused than ever, I felt as if John was helping me make huge leaps towards getting my revenge. I was ready to go after them now.

"Hey, kid." John had just come into the study to meet me at the table. He had a few books in one hand, and was holding an ice pack on his face with the other. "Since you've gotten so adept at kicking my ass lately, I figured we could do some school lessons today." I didn't even look up. I was aggravated and ready to take out my emotions on these *things* John was claiming were possible. "You awake inside there, kid?"

"Yeah," I said as I slid my chair away from the desk top and got up to walk past him out of the door. "I just don't see why I should sit in here and read when we could go get the fuckers who burnt down my house now."

"Listen Cole, not everything comes to fruition overnight." John was staring at me intensely as he blocked the doorway.

"Move," I stated. I was beginning to get angry now.

"Where you gonna go, Cole? Did you think about that?" John's voice was raising as he put his hand on my chest and pushed me backwards. "You think you're ready to go after an entire coven of witches just because you've been whipping up on

an old man, huh?

You have no idea what it is going to be like, kid."

"You have no idea what it is like you dick!" I was

fuming now. John had a look of confusion on his face as I moved

toward him to continue. "My house isn't just gone, man. It isn't

the fact that all my stuff was there and all my material things are

gone. My fucking best friend is gone. I have to live with that

every day. There's a hole growing bigger and darker inside my

heart all the time. And the people responsible have burned my

house down because I stumbled upon them in a drunken and high

stupor." I was shaking. It felt like forever since I had talked about

Ty. Everything had been building up and building up and I was

just exploding, and John was the thing standing in the way of me.

Suddenly I felt my bottom lip start to quiver as our eyes met again,

"I miss him man," I said as I bowed my head and hid the tears with

my hand.

John stepped up and put his arm around me. We stood

there together for what seemed like an eternity until I could calm myself down. "Cole, there's so much you don't know yet," John began, "This isn't just a group of townspeople in white robes in the night, it is a group of evil people who have been meeting in secret to worship the devil. They do Satan's deeds, kid. I want you to realize that, and let it sink in that demons and the devil are not just words or names of characters in the Bible, but that they are out there, and have directly affected your life." He patted me twice on the back and looked in to my eyes with grave sincerity as he began again, "I want revenge for you, Cole. I promise you if you stick with me, you will learn everything you need to get it, and I will do all that I can to help you see it through, kid." His voice was low and deep. I stood up straight and collected myself giving him a nod of confirmation. "Good," I stated, "Now let's get back to work."

Three long months have gone by. Ninety days of training, reading, researching, and focusing in on how to find out who exactly was behind this coven. I felt different. Between the fear, the guilt, and the whiskey fueled rage I had changed for good. I was ready. And the revelation couldn't be coming at a better time. Tonight was the night John promised we would go back to the woods.

After spending most of the day pacing and drinking, I stepped inside to the study to sit down with John. He looked up from his glass with a nod and a grin, inviting me to sit. We sat together for a minute or two, just the silence and whiskey. Then, as John lit a cigarette, he looked at me and began to say something.

"This is it, kid. You're ready. Tonight is the night we start to close the gap on these bastards." I answered with a smirk and a light of my own Marlboro. It seemed at points over the past ninety days that I would never hear those words. It was almost surreal for it all to be coming to fruition tonight. All the pain, the torture, research, training, isolation, the drugs, alcohol, and tears were going to be worth it.

"It feels weird to hear you say that," I responded while exhaling a cloud of smoke. "These past few months I've been insisting with you that I was ready, every day, and your stubborn old ass is finally agreeing."

"Old?" John laughed as he continued, "well you got it all right, kid. We are ready. You're ready. I am old. Too damn old." He took another swig of bourbon and cleared his throat to begin again. "I just want you to know, this is a marathon, kid. We are at war here. Don't go in thinking we win it all tonight. Small steps, small steps."

"Yeah, we'll see about all that after tonight." There was no way I was going to let them off. Three months of waiting, if I had a chance, whoever was behind this was mine.

"I've created a monster in you, you know that?" John said as he shook his head and put out his cigarette. "Oh, and one more thing," he started as he looked up at me from the ashtray, "Your lazy ass ever finish sharpening up that old mauler?"

"Uh, yeah I did. I double edged it just like you said, why?" John smiled at my answer. It was strange to me that he was bringing it up now. I almost forgot about that old thing; I was starting to think I'd never get a chance to use it how I intended.

"Good, kid. Get that hickory handle we made for it and put it back together tonight before we leave. By the time you come back in, I'll have the Camaro loaded, and then we can talk about how to go about killing all the different evil pricks we might start coming across after tonight." I nodded as I walked out the door to the barn where I kept the mauler and the handle. What did John mean by 'how to go about killing them'? Wasn't the combat skills enough? I sat down and began to reconstruct a once innocent tool into a killing machine as my mind meandered through the prospects of what in the hell I had actually gotten myself into. As the sun set, I finished the product, held it up smiling, and began to walk back towards the manor.

The Fight Begins Tonight

John slammed the trunk on the Camaro as I approached. "Come inside, kid" he said as he motioned toward the manor. "I got some shit laid out to show you, you've still got a little to learn before we take off." I followed him in as I tried to prepare myself for what might be next.

I followed him into the study where a table full of various killing devices lay in front of me. I studied over the table, looking at a couple machetes, a few knives, two guns, and a couple of homemade Molotov Cocktail looking bottles. Taken back a little, I looked toward John for some kind of explanation.

"These are things you need to be very familiar with kid." John stared intently at the table while he continued, "Witches, for all intensive purposes, are human beings. They may be rotten, lying, devil worshiping humans, but they are only humans. Anything that can kill us will kill them."

"So why the overkill with the machetes and whatever is in those bottles?"

"Well, the church taught persecutors of witches to use a more permanent method of killing witches to ensure they were dead besides a simple gunshot or stab wound." He lifted up the machete and started, "They preferred a beheading. Hence the overkill."

"Damn, that is about as personal as it gets." I was overwhelmed with the idea of having to cut someone's head off. I mean I know it has to be done but that is an all-new level of revenge and anger even for me.

"What they did to you was personal too, Cole. Don't forget that." He was right. I nodded in agreement as the thought of the past few months was making the beheading thing a lot easier to swallow. Making his way to the other side of the table, John grabbed the guns.

"I bet you're wondering why I have guns laid out if what I told you just now is true, aren't you?"

"A little bit, yeah" I answered with a smile.

"These aren't actually guns, Cole. Well, they are, but they shoot flares, not bullets. You see, while a beheading is very personal, everyone knows the old stories of witches being burned at the stake."

"Well, that explains the rest of the table's contents then," I said motioning to the cocktail bottles.

"Sharp kid." John said with a laugh. "So that's basically the gist of it. Burn them if you can, they hate that, and if you can't; cut the bastard's head off." I nodded with affirmation, picking up one of his knives and smirking.

"What?" John asked.

"Nothing, it's just that you call this a knife." I laughed as I pulled my bone handle from its sheath at my side, laughing.

"Very funny, kid. Very funny. Can we just hit the road now?" I nodded, still laughing as I held the door motioning him through. Tonight was the beginning of the end for this hell that I have been living through.

No words were said on the ride to the cemetery, just the sound of a humming Chevy 327 and the light from the moon hanging high and full in the sky. John drove by slowly, checking everything out carefully before making a plan. After driving back around to the old shiner trail on the ridge behind the cemetery, we decided to park and start our trek from there. I strapped a machete to my back, and a flare gun to my boot to accompany my bone handle knife, and john took the rest of the weapons. I shut the trunk as I followed this stranger become friend into the stale night air and an uncertain future.

As we made our way further through the cemetery towards the tree line, the smell of fire and incense began to fill the air. A sinister fog was rising just to the top of the headstones, setting the tone for what was to come. Standing on the verge of the woods now, John stopped and peered back at me.

"Just remember everything, kid." His eyes were sincere and voice unshaken. "Remember it all, Cole. Remember all that has happened; all you've lost. Remember everything you picked up from me in the past three months, and remember to focus. Pick your spots, kid. This is war, it ain't no sprint." I stood there, flashing back on everything that had happened. I thought about Ty dying, the fire, and how I lost Katie because of my own demons, literal and metaphorical. I accepted my past and what lay ahead just beyond these trees for my near future with a sigh and prepared to follow John into the woods.

With each step the sounds and sights became increasingly telling of the gruesome scene we were inevitably going to come upon. The glow from the gigantic fire flickered high into the treetops rivaling the moonlight. The faint sounds of chanting in some foreign tongue grew in strength by the yard. The sound of dancing and the music of the damned was now audible.

John motioned over to a rise in the land between thick bush and we made our way there to hide and observe. From our spot behind the knoll we could see the witches in all their macabre glory. Everyone was naked. All the women at the fire were old, like buried for 100 years old. The few men that were there were naked as well, but cloaked in the fur of goats. One's leading the procession with a flute. They danced and sang and followed the piper around the fire for what seemed like forever, before suddenly stopping and sitting by the fire opposite the piper and his goat men.

They walked over to a wooden table where they began to pray in tongues to a most certainly ungodly evil.

"Latin." John whispered in my direction as they continued what was almost certainly some type of mass. Thunder rolled in the distance as we both turned to see what the coven would do next. The one that was leading was preaching vigorously along, with his gruesome disciples annunciating responses on their ques. One of the other men clad in goats fur brought over a large deep bowl to the alter. The Piper and he bowed at each other before he took the bowl from his assistant; holding it high for all the witches to see.

"What the hell is that?"

"I'm not sure, but it looks like some kind of offering; kind of like the bread and wine in the church. God only knows what is in this one though." The fact that John didn't even know for sure what was in the bowl gave me chills. I was beginning to feel as if we shouldn't be here; like we were overwhelmingly in over our heads. The thunder was inching closer and the wind had picked up vastly. A pungent aroma filled the air.

"Should we make a move or something?" I didn't want to even hear an answer to what I was asking, although I felt I needed to ask.

"No, kid. Marathon, not a sprint, remember?" John began looked towards me and crouched lower behind the knoll to better hide the conversation. I joined his stance as he continued. "Listen, kid. And remember everything you hear and see. It is just as important to know your enemy as it is to know how to kill them. We gotta understand the why."

"To be honest, I was hoping you would say that." We laughed as we moved back toward the upper part of the knoll. Lightening flashed for the first time. A storm was moving in on us fast. In the light of the flash, I could see the faces of the people in front of us for the first time. All of them looked familiar. The men's identity was saved by the animal fur coverings, but the naked women's faces shone like eerie ancient statues.

I began to creep up over the knoll to get closer. I had to know more. What was in that bowl? Who exactly were these people out here in the woods of my town? I looked back at John and to my surprise, he was reluctantly following me. Taking each step carefully, I meandered from tree to tree doing my best ninja impression. Finally reaching a massive oak, I was close enough to make out faces and acute details. The women were now lining up and one by one proceeding to the men. I could see the piper's lower body now, and he had the legs of a goat; tail and all. He was wearing a hooded cloak, with horns stuck through the top, and nothing of the face showing except the piercing glow of his eyes.

As the women began to make their way to the alter, I intensely watched every move. They were bowing at the alter towards whatever was in that bowl, and then proceeding towards the piper himself, and kissing him. Not just anywhere were they kissing, though; but they all kissed him on his buttocks. Only God knows why, but they did.

After I got over what exactly it was that I was watching unfold, I started paying attention to things. Like there were two men with the piper, both shorter, but I could swear the one on the right was young-like my age young. He was almost familiar in his mannerisms. *I knew him* from the way he moved. As for the women, I was staring at faces now. Unmistakable defining features, and I was rattled by what I saw. The first several that skipped their way up the unholy line to grovel at the feet of the piper held no merit. It was the few anchors of the evil coven, however; that caught me. Right in front of me stood the hags from the pub that day who were surrounding Katie. I could've pointed them out in a crowed of a thousand. Their corroded, evil, and weathered faces were engraved in my mind. I watched them gallivant along leading the pack from the rear with sheer joy in their eyes. Something about seeing that amount of elation and evil simultaneously struck fear into my soul. They were from all over this town. Where is John anyway?

As I looked over my shoulder to locate him, a strange and sudden silence that overtook the woods. Even the sounds from the fire were non existant. The hairs on the back of my neck were at attention. John was nowhere to be seen and I am too afraid to look back towards the fire. I needed to find him. With a single step, the cracking of a stray branch sang an echoing alarm to all the creatures of the night that I was there; an unwelcomed guest to their freak show. I was had. *Where the fuck was John?!*

Lightening flashed intensely, lighting up the landscape and enlightening the fear on my face. In that moment, the piercing eyes of the piper shone to mine, and connected directly. Like an off switch on a light, the lightening subdued and the piper was not visible. None of them were. I began to run. Faster and more efficient than I ever had in my young life. All around me were the sounds of shrewd laughter and maniacal screams. The rustling sounds from the bush showed off the swift movement leading to my inevitable demise. The metaphorical walls were closing in. As I feared for what lye ahead, I noticed myself moving ever closer to the tree line opening to the cemetery. Above all the ungodly chaos and my own panting, I could hear an engine. That bastard was *waiting* on me.

Within a few feet now, I could almost feel the monsters touching me. Their sinful breath beat down upon the back of my neck. I could feel the sharp grip of something on my left shoulder.

With a rip and a tear, I made it through. I turned around to see what followed, and to my surprise; nothing. Pairs and pairs of eyes glowed on me. Sinister growls came from behind the tree line but for the time being, I was safe. It was weird though; almost as if they wanted it that way.

"C'mon kid, let's haul ass!" Hollered John from his front row seat inside the Camaro. His voice drew my attention away from those unholy woods and back to survival. I slouched into the Camaro with a slam as we sped off, living to hunt witches another night.

One Is The Loneliest Number

The sight of the Long gravel driveway leading to the manor was a beautiful sight after all that we had been through last night. Sunlight shined through the windshield of the Camaro as we parked. It was serene. I could finally breathe again-and with that piece came a jolt of memory; John fucking left me last night. Anger was washing over me as I stepped out of the car with a slam waiting for John to follow me.

"So where the hell were you last night?" John was staring at me with a grin as I questioned him. "Seriously man, what the fuck? Shit gets real and I have to worry about where you are? You almost got me killed!"

"Don't be so dramatic, sweetheart. You want to know what I was doing? I was saving our asses, that's what I was doing." I stopped. Was he being serious right now? He got me into this crap and when it actually started to go down, he was gone. He was, however; ready and waiting on me in the Camaro so maybe he had a point. I don't know what to think. John was looking at me waiting on a response. There wasn't going to be one.

"Well, that's it, huh?" John continued as I stand here struck with a billion thoughts in my mind. "Boy, you came out of the gate awful hard, but once the shit got a little deep you got pretty quiet, kid. Since you're in the listening mood, let me explain myself from last night." I hope he is telling the truth. I didn't follow this goddamn yahoo's every order for months to have it all come out to be a load of crap. "Last night, when you started to move forward, I thought you were crazy."

"Gee thanks a lot!"

"Anytime. Anyways, I started to follow you reluctantly, and I noticed something."

"What was it?"

"I don't know… it was this feeling."

"A *feeling,* John? A fucking *feeling?!* Well your feeling almost got me killed!"

"Yeah, I had a *feeling* smartass, and without it you would've been dead for sure."

"Well, please explain then." John sneered at me with distain for mocking him but continued nonetheless.

"What you were doing, it felt too easy. It felt to me like they wanted you to be watching ya know? Like the closer you got, the better it fit their needs. So I went backtracking to see if we missed anything that would point to them knowing you were there."

"Did you find anything?"

"More than I intended to, kid. On my way back I heard a rustling, and then before I knew it, a girl was swiftly running around me, on all sides to confuse me. As my eyes tried to catch up, she suddenly appeared in front of me. She was cloaked in darkness, so the only detail I could make out was that she was a lot younger than the rest of them."

"So what happened next? How the hell did you get out of that unscathed?"

"I didn't think I was going to. She was snarling at me, and began to walk slowly towards me. I flashed my machete and held my flare gun aimed at her heart and advised her not to make another move, and she stopped."

"She just stopped?"

"Well, no…she grabbed the barrel of the gun and stuck it on her forehead. She said there was nothing there where I was aiming and that this would be better. Then she smiled and backed away saying that I wasn't the one she was after that night."

"She was talking about me?"

"Yeah. And after that, she was gone. So I hauled ass out of there to get the Camaro ready trusting that you paid enough attention to what I told you to save your own bacon; or at least get it to the tree line so I could." If my mind wasn't swimming before, it definitely was now.

"I guess I owe you, then."

"No, kid you don't."

"What?"

"You did just as much as me, Cole. Your instincts are great. You knew when to pick your spots; when to stay, when to run; and where to run. And I'm betting you saw plenty of key things in that time that I distracted the little lady, right?"

"Actually yeah. I saw some familiar faces as far as the witches go. I don't really know how much that helps except for the fact that I know who I'm talking about fighting now."

"I figured the witches would be local. Witches are old and rooted in the towns where they committed to the devil, but there are some exceptions to that so I'm glad you got proof of it."

"Yeah. And I didn't see the younger female, but I did notice that one of the men helping the mass leader was young."
"Like how young are we talking?"

"Like my age young. He looked like a kid out there compared to the rest of them. And even more so, I couldn't shake this feeling that I knew him. Just the way he was moving and his body language; it was like I had known him my whole life." I could tell John's mind was turning now. Ideas were running through his mind quick as a whip and I wanted in on them. "What is it man? You look like that means something."

"It's just that I've been following your high school, Cole. And a kid at these masses kind of makes sense in a lot of ways."

"What do you mean?"

"Well, the way these covens stay strong is sacrificing to the demon, right?"

"Right..."

"What I'm saying is, this isn't necessarily just about you here. Three boys and a girl have gone missing from Eden and the surrounding three counties since Ty was murdered. Usually sacrifices are centered around babies but for some reason it looks like these witches are settling for teens." This was HUGE. So Ty wasn't killed as a way to get to me? But why him? And why am I the one to stop it? This is all becoming overwhelming.

"Three boys and a girl?" I asked.

"Yeah."

"Got any names?"

"No, Cole. We aren't ready to get back in the game like that yet. There is still questions we need to answer first."

"No disrespect, but you're the one who kept this from me. And if this is all true, then I have someone to check on. You might not understand, but I need you to trust me, here."

"I do trust you. But before I let you run off and play John Wayne, you need to hear the rest of it."

"I'm listening."

"Okay. So the reason a teen being at the masses makes sense is he could be their inside ticket. He is one of them but also one of the kids, do you see what I mean?"

"Yeah. It's fucked up but I get it."

"Listen, If we are right here, then this kid could be anyone. Everyone is a potential victim and every boy is a suspect. You have to be on your game at all times when you go to check on whoever it is you're checking on."

"I understand. I got it. And I think I have a short list of potential suspects myself."

"Just be careful. And if you can, Stop back by the cemetery and see if you can find anything pointing to the cult taking these teens. In the daylight you will be more than safe, just make it a quick sweep."

"Sure thing."

"Remember, careful. You aren't any good to me dead."

"I know, I got it. I'll be back as soon as I can." John nodded and let me on my way. I loaded my smaller knives in my leather bag on the Harley and my bowie on my side and took off towards town.

The more I was thinking about what John said on the way to town, the more I came to one conclusion: Blake. It all fit together. Kids were missing from the high school, a young male my age was at the mass in the woods, and he was the best example of evil I had at that age. I was starting to see red with every dot I connected. It was he. It had to be. Priority number one was making sure Katie is okay, but God help the man who gets in the way of me and Blake.

The miles passed quickly, and before I knew it, I was pulling into the parking lot at the school. As I stepped off my bike, calmness washed over me. I had two tasks here, and I was focused. With tunnel vision in full effect, I made my way to the main entrance. I pushed my way through the halls upon entering, ignoring the various waves and greetings. It was passing period, or in other words, 5 minutes of mass hysteria. I scanned the crowd for Katie as I fought my way towards her locker. Text books and rude shoulders bounced off me, nearly claiming my leather jacket at points on the way. And then, about fifteen feet from her locker, I stopped. There she was, preparing for the next class. She seemed fine, just as beautiful as I remembered-maybe even more so. Just as I began to make my way over to talk to her, so did someone else-Blake.

I saw Red. All objectives and all that focus disappeared faster from me than a blink of an eye. I covered that fifteen feet in what must have been a millisecond and met Blake at full speed; and he met the lockers. I held him there with my forearm. The shock and fear was evident on his face. His eyes widened as I began to swing with my left hand. Punch after punch, I started to go physically and mentally numb. I could feel the moisture from the blood on my fist, but not the action of hitting. The numbness had overtaken me. Pairs and pairs of hands over came me and started forcing my body away from his. Just before they broke me to the ground and freed the bastard, I leaned in and said, "I know about you. If you pick her next I swear I'll kill you." I couldn't fight the hands anymore and I let them pull me to the ground. Katie's screams were audible in the background as they drug me into the office to contain me.

As I sat in the office of my old high school, the numbness began to wear away. I could feel the sting of the cuts on my knuckles, accompanied by the inflammation and swelling starting to take place. The anger was returning in full force as well. I should've finished the job. They had no idea what he was doing out there. I was *saving* them. The principle motioned me back into his private office with a stern look in his eyes. I complied and followed him in closing the door behind me.

"Just what the hell was that, Cole?" the level of heat in his voice towards me was serious. He was serious.

"I don't have to explain myself to you."

"Trust me, this is going to be easier on you if you do. The police are on their way here now. Statements are being taken as we speak. Cole, you could've killed Blake."

"No offense, but I'm not the killer here."

"What is that supposed to mean?"

"Nothing. I was saving her man. I had to."

"Saving who, Cole?"

"Me…he was trying to protect me." A voice came from the entrance accompanied by the opening of the office door. It was Katie.

"Katie, sit down in here and close that damn door." He was livid now. Nobody was allowed to interrupt his meetings that way. "Now, you better have a damn good explanation behind waltzing into my office during a very important matter like this one."

"I do." she continued, "Like I said, he was protecting me." I looked at Katie somewhat confused. We hadn't talked in so long but I could tell she had a plan here, I just couldn't figure out what it was. "You see," she started again, "Blake and I have a history, and I had recently filed a restraining order against him as you should know." I was speechless. Did she really have a restraining order? What did the idiot do now? Did she know about what I knew?

"Yes, I am aware Katie. But what does that have to do with Cole?"

"Well if you recall, Blake is not supposed to be within 200 feet of me, at any time, even in here. When Cole came up to me, Blake was close enough to touch me. He was just defending me."

"Be that as it may, Cole was excessive and publicly assaulted a student of mine."

"No, Cole assaulted an 18 year old man who was abusive and forced himself on me. As much as you may want to cover that up to protect your football season, the courts are on my side here, and if you don't believe me wait until the officers are here." Wow. I couldn't believe everything I had missed around here. I knew Blake was an ass, but hitting Katie?? Either way, I needed to get out of here while the getting was good, or at least possible.

"Besides, Mr. Principle, what are you going to do? You can't expel him, he graduated early." The look on his face was priceless. Katie had stumped him totally. He vigorously rubbed his head, searching for an answer.

"Just get out of my sight," he stated. "Get out now before the officials come here and we all regret what just happened."

"Yes sir, no complaints from me." I collected myself to stand up and leave when Katie spoke up.

"Sir, I'd like to leave for the rest of the day. Cole will take me home, right Cole?"

"Yeah, sure thing." The steam was leaking from all points of entry on the principle's head. He was about to blow.

"Just go. Both of you." Katie went to grab her things from her locker and said she would meet me out in the lot. As I walked out to my bike, I passed by the nurse station and saw Blake being wheeled out. He was holding an ice pack on one side of his face, the other was so stained of crimson you could hardly make him out. His collar was torn and the blood stains continued well onto his shirt. I felt weird walking by my own doing like that, but I felt no guilt. He deserved it for what he did to these kids, if it was him. Moreover, he deserved it for ever touching someone like Katie. I stood and watched as they wheeled him towards the back exit and then I made my way outside to the parking lot.

After a few minutes of waiting leaned up against my motorcycle, Katie walked up to me. There was worry in her eyes as she started to address me. "Where have you been, Cole? And is this really how you show up after months?"

"Katie, the last time I tried to talk to you, my best friend had just died and you called me an addict. I don't owe you an explanation on where I've been."

"And what about Blake?"

"I've been doing a lot of looking into things, Katie. With the help of a new friend of mine, we have made a lot of progress in finding out what really happened to Ty." A new fear lit up her eyes as I was talking.

"Cole, It was a suicide. That's it. You *have* to let this go."

"Really, Katie? What about the rest of these kids that have gone missing from here in the past few months? Suicides too, or are they just runaways?"

"How did you hear about that?"

"My friend told me today. I came back because for one, I had a one person suspect list, and I wanted to make sure you were okay."

"Well how noble of you. So let me guess, you just killed two birds with one stone in there, that's why it was so brutal wasn't it?"

"Something like that. Agree or disagree, I saved your ass in there, and maybe a bunch of other kids in the process."

"Cole, you didn't save any kids. Blake isn't some kind of killer, and you aren't anyone's hero. Don't try to spin this around."

"Did he really hit you?" Her expression changed to a heavy one.

"Yeah. Not long after you disappeared, Blake started to change."

"Change how?"

"Not how you think, Cole. He was an ass. Towards me, mostly. We had grown distant, and I was thinking of leaving him when I found out he had been cheating on me with my friend, Destiny."

"Oh. I'm sorry."

"I'm sure. Anyways when I tried dumping him, he started leaving his mark. Black eyes, bruises on my arms, that kind of thing."

"What did you do?"

"Well, for a long time, I was just scared. Eventually it got to the point I thought he might take it too far, so I went to see Addison Miller."

"Did you tell your parents?"

"No. Actually Addison thought that might be a bad idea, he said my dad might try to take matters into his own hands."

"Oh…"

"Yeah. So anyways for the past month or so, I have been trying to get the school to suspend him from the campus or something due to my restraining order but they have been dodging it, and Addison hasn't been too much help. Then you showed up today."

"And killed two birds with one stone." She shot me a scolding look. "Listen, I'm sorry that had to happen to you, you could've called me you know?"

"No, I couldn't. Cole, you can't even take care of yourself; how would you be able to help me?"

"Well, I think I did a fair job today." She shook her head in disgust.

"Cole, you are on a dark path. The last I heard from you, you were blaming a fairy tale for your best friends death and your blood could've been bottled and sold as premium whiskey. If you want to save someone save yourself."

"Katie, it's the *truth*. I don't know if I will ever be able to prove that to you, but if I can save you from it, that is the most important thing."

"Cole, I called my mother on the way out here. I suggest you leave and head back wherever it is you have been." Her voice was cutting right through me. It was vicious and cold. "I don't want to see you until you've accepted some things." I nodded angrily as I grabbed my helmet and got on my bike.

"You know one of these times, I'm gonna be able to say it was nice to see you, Katie." I smiled as I continued, "The funny part about it is, even though I know its gonna end up this way, I still dream about getting to see you again." She spoke not a word and turned away as I started the Harley and made my way out of the school parking lot.

I drove up to the cemetery and passed by to make sure it was empty. Once I was clear, I drove through and up to the wood line. I walked the trails back to where I remembered the mass going down. The smell of burnt incense was prominent as I walked through the area looking for a sign that it actually happened. The alter was gone, and the circle was covered up where the fire had been. Looking down, just about in the middle of where that circle had been, I saw the corner of something sticking out of the dirt. Bending down to pick it up, I realized it was a license. I pulled it out of the dirt and brushed it off. The name on the license read George A Towns. George was undoubtedly one of the boys missing that John had mentioned. He was from the class below mine. The further I dug through the dirt, the more interesting this little adventure got. I found a bowl, a few small scattered bones, and one class ring that belonged to a new transfer student, Damien Covington. Poor bastard must have picked the worst possible time to move towns. I collected my findings and headed back to John's manor.

Everything was oddly quiet as I pulled up and shut off the Harley. I looked for signs of life outside and saw nothing except a black cat scurrying from the house out through the garden. John must be inside. I grabbed everything that I had found out of my leather bag on the front forks and headed for the door. The Camaro hadn't moved since I had been gone. As I walked up the stairs, I noticed the door wasn't latched all the way. It wasn't enough to see light to the inside, but just enough to not be shut all the way. This was strange.

"John?" I called out as I opened the door and started to enter, "You too drunk to latch the door?" No answer. As I stepped through the door way my eyes were drawn to the study. The door to it was swung completely open, and I could see that it had been rummaged through. A feeling of worry rushed over me. I walked in and sat down my findings to investigate. It looked like John had been violently searching for something. But what? This is his study, what could possibly be so hidden from him? The more I wandered through the room, the stranger I felt. Wherever John was in this house, I'm sure he had an answer. As I stepped out of the study, I noticed one of John's leather harness boots lay at the side of the stairs. Now I was getting goosebumps. John isn't a take of your shoes kinda guy. His study was never ransacked like that, and he was *never* this quiet. Then, as I walked back around to the front face of the stairs, I looked up. I wish to God I hadn't, but there I was, and my answer was staring me in the face. John was hanging there, lifeless, from the old chandelier at the top of the grand stairway. Inside my mind I was exploding. As much as I wanted to scream or yell or do *something,* all I could muster was the hair on the back of my neck standing up, and a single tear down the side of my cheek.

After a lifetime of trying, I gathered enough courage to climb the stairs to let him down. With each step, I broke down a little more. When I made it to the top, I struggled some, but eventually got the rope cut and lay him down gently. His wrists were both slit almost to the bone. Did John really do this? I finally bought into this crazy ass game and he was the only thing I had. He was the only one I had. It wasn't a whole lot, but he was my only friend. I wiped a tear away from my eye and noticed a stool about three feet over from us. It had been kicked over, presumably by John. I leaned up and with two fingers gently closed his eyelids as I moved over to the stool. On the back side of the stool, partially stuck under its seat, was a blood stained piece of notebook paper. Cautiously, I picked it up, turned it over, and read its haunting words:

Cole,

You know I've got my secrets, And before I go, I need to tell you one more. A long time ago, before I chased witches around this damn country, I was nothing more than a father. I was a husband and a father to a handsome baby boy. Cole, I know you may have grown up harsh, and maybe you hated life without a father, but I want to let you know, I am so proud to call you my son. Don't be afraid to walk in my footsteps, it's a good path. There is more, but you'll find out later. Son, don't be afraid to continue without me. I'm a damaged man, and besides, you did it your whole life.

-J

Tears began to accompany the bloodstains on this paper. After everything, all that I've had to endure, I meet my father but only in death. He strung me along, showing me his ways, and then left me alone, *again.* This time, though, it was forever. Could this be true? I had no way of proving or disproving it. My mother died years and years ago, my grandfather was gone, too. And now, the man claiming to be my long lost father was dead, too. Too much. This was way, *way* too much.

I made my way outside and put together all of the things we had used into the trunk of the Camaro, just so the police wouldn't find it later. I took a few of the books he had shown me, one of them being the Key of Solomon. Once the trunk was loaded, I closed it shut, and sat right there, on the hood of my fathers Camaro, and waited for the authorities to come and pull him out of this old manor in a body bag.

They showed up quickly, and after my statement I stuck around just long enough to watch an ominous black bag be wheeled out on a gurney. I had to get away. My life, especially these past few months, was boiling over in my mind. I thanked the responders, said I would be in touch if needed, and then I fired up the old Camaro and left Eden in the rearview with a cloud of dust.

I lay my boot full into the pedal of the Camaro until Eden was a long gone thought in my mind. No matter how far I drive, though, the memories were banging loud in my head. I need a drink. *Welcome to Danville* read the nearest sign I passed by at an unhealthy speed. Danville it was. I slowed down to find the nearest watering hole and tap the keg myself. Two lefts and a right across the railroad tracks on main, and I was there. Danville Crossings Bar and Grill. It was a quaint place. The whole town was. The building seemed inviting and homey, despite its rather large size. I pulled into the gravel lot and found an empty spot after some time searching, and made my way to the door. Gimme Three Steps shook the floor of the front porch as I grabbed the handle to the entrance. I meandered my way to the bar running the entire length of the back wall and found a stool.

"What can I getcha, sweetie?" The bartender's attitude, among other things, was perky and enjoyable.

"Crown on the rocks. Leave the bottle, sugar." She smiled as she reached for the bottle to fufill my order. Her blonde hair accented hazel eyes very well, and her tank top, pulled up just above a navel ring, brought to the forefront her curves and didn't hurt the tip jar I'm sure.

"One crown on the rocks. And I'll sit you a bottle right here tough guy, just try to save some for the rest of us okay?"

"Yes ma'am, you got it." She winked as she made her way down the bar to get other orders. I picked up my whiskey and wished I had her outlook on life. That was over now for me, the curtains were drawn back and the fun was gone. It had been for a while now. As time passed, one bottle turned into a second, which the cute little bartender made clear was more than enough. I was numbing more and more by the sip now. My vision was blurred, but the memories of what I left behind was still grippingly haunting me. Then, in a break between the songs, I felt a hand on my shoulder and a familiar voice serenaded my ears.

"Hey, stranger. Fancy running into you here." I turned to see, and it was Elaine. Surprised, I took a minute to process before my rebuttle.

"Well look who it is. What the hell are you doing out this way?"

"Running, just like you I suppose." I smirked as I took another drink.

"How have you been since Ty?"

"Lost. Empty. I only stayed for a few weeks before I was drowning, and then my uncle turned me on to this town. I'm staying in a rental of his a few blocks down until I get back on my feet again."

"Yeah, I hear ya. Everything was just overflowing for me after Ty and I just had to go. This just happened to be the first stop on the map." I looked into her eyes and felt a little peace. It was nice to talk to someone who knew what I felt like, even if she didn't know it all. "I'm glad you were here, Elaine. I needed to open up a little."

"Well, Cole, I'd say by the bottles here you've opened up more than a little. You shouldn't be driving anywhere tonight."

"I think I'll be okay. This is busch league for me, ya know."

"Yeah, I know, but I'm serious. Come to my apartment. Play it close to the vest just for tonight. I have a bunch of Ty's old things that I have been too afraid to go through alone; we could sit and do it together. I know you don't owe me and we were never even close, but this would really be good for me, Cole. It might be good for both of us." Her words comforted me. This kind of thing wasn't usually my style but she was right. At least it felt right. It might be the idea, maybe the whiskey, but God, it felt right.

"Okay, Elaine. You got me. I'm coming home with you." She put her hand on my shoulder and smiled as I continued, "I hope your plan doesn't end there." We shared a laugh as I let her lead the way out of the bar towards her apartment.

After a short walk through downtown Dansville, we made it to her door. Looking back at me with a grin, she unlocked it and led the way. I followed her in and sat on the couch in the living room as she turned on the lights. She turned on the radio-classic rock. Zeppelin played soft in the background as she joined me on the couch. She sat two beers down on the table, gesturing one to me. I could hardly see straight as it was, but I accepted.

She walked across the room, dancing to the music, and grabbed a box.

"I love this song." She stated as she looked back towards me. I nodded in affirmation. If I didn't 'love' it before, it sure was growing on me all the sudden.

"What's in the box?" I asked, doing my best Seven impression. She smiled and rolled her eyes, shooting me a look. "What?" I asked.

"Nothing...You and Ty really were best friends, weren't you?"

"Yeah. What makes you ask?"

"The music. The quotes. The insane tolerance for liquor. It's like you were twins." She laughed as she grabbed the box and made her way back over. "This is the box of his stuff. Mostly just old concert tickets from you guys back in the day that he had kept, a few pictures, and some other old junk." Her voice was just background noise as I got lost in the box. It was like Ty was there again. His favorite lighter, a red Bic. All the ticket stubs from the concerts we had seen over the years. I missed him so much. I looked up and she was staring just as intently at their

picture from last years prom.

"It's surreal isn't it?"

"Yeah, it is." Her eyes moved from the picture and

fixated on mine. Bad Company now gently serenaded the radio.

In this moment I noticed something. I wasn't here for Ty, as weird

as it was to admit, I was here for Elaine.

She sat their picture back down on the table as she

moved in close to me. My hand touched hers as Ready for Love

tempted us to go further. I moved my hand from hers up her arm

and neck to her cheek, running the tips of my fingers across her

soft skin and caressing her cheek. Her hands wandered on my

body, across my shoulders and arms as I slid my hand to the back

of her head and pulled her in for a kiss. With one great, slow kiss,

the fire was started. Nothing was soft anymore. I laid her back

and mounted her as we continued to kiss passionately. Her hands

glided up down my torso and slipped underneath my shirt. She

firmly felt my abs, running her hands slowly along each curve and divot. Then, they swiftly moved to the ends of my shirt and ripped it the rest of the way over my head.

Our bodies moved in rhythm with the music as we undressed each other further. Goosebumps sprouted furiously across my skin as Elaine bit my lip between kisses. It was strange, but for once, my mind wasn't filled with hate or anger. It wasn't filled with thoughts of revenge or sadness, it wasn't filled with plans on my next move. As a matter of fact, it wasn't filled at all. It was devoid save for one emotion; lust. I wanted something besides an answer for the first time in a long time, and it was her. I wrapped my arms around her and lifted her up to carry her to the bedroom. The feeling of her fingers running through my hair excited me. The neck kisses brought on an eruption of emotion as we made it into her bedroom.

I sat her on the bed and she brought herself to her knees, smiling as she finished undressing herself. Somehow, she was even more intoxicating. She moved closer to me, pressing her lips to my body and grabbing my boxers, slowly pulling down. Her eyes burned through mine straight into my soul as she began to put her lips on the shaft of my erection, subtly but firmly sucking. My body was beginning to shake as she continued. Her bottom lip drug across my abdominal muscles as she kissed her way back up to me, looking deeply into my eyes. I don't know if it was the copious amounts of alcohol I had consumed or the amazing erotica I was experiencing, but the room was spinning. Her hands were gripped firmly around my neck as she pulled me onto the bed to join her. Then, Elaine pulled away a bit as she threw me down onto the bed and climbed on top.

Her hands ran over mine, nails dragging along my skin. She held my arms above my head, our hands clinched tightly together. Her hips moved on mine, keeping pace with the radio. She sped up and slowed down, adjusting to what pleased me the most, and never let me have too much control. Her hands now moved back to my neck asphyxiating me as she leaned in and whispered, "It's time for you to come for me." My entire body tensed up as I soaked up every bit of what she was giving to me. She squeezed tighter and tighter as she began to ride me faster and harder. I was beginning to get light headed. With each thrust, I was closer and closer. "I can feel you're close," she whispered as she bent down to my ear. She was riding even faster yet. My heart was racing. She stayed low and close, breathing heavily by my ear as she choked tighter. Then, she slowed to a crawl, seductively taking her time with each stroke, tightening herself around me on the way down. I was shaking vigorously, and couldn't hold on any longer. I pulled her close, digging my hands into her back. She bit my earlobe and let out a loud moan as I pushed deep and finished. She smiled as she moved off to my side and kissed my chest before laying her head down. As weird as it was, it felt right. For an instance, my life felt *aligned.* Weird or not, there were two things I was sure of tonight: I was going to get a good nights sleep for once, and it was a night I would never forget.

Witchy Woman

A chilling breeze sliced through me and woke me from a sleep I must have undertaken. The room was still black, insinuating it was still night. With a long stretch, I brought my hands up to rub my eyes and adjust them to the darkness of the room. A window to my left was open, curtains swaying freely in the night wind. That explained the cold breeze. It hadn't hit me until now, but it was silent. No sounds from outside, and no sounds from the person who should be next to me. *Where was Elaine?*

Just as I grabbed the satin sheet and shifted to get up and look for her, a howling hurricane force wind shot through the window. A black figure rode in on the wind gust and overtook me, shoving me back into the mattress. I couldn't move or talk. I was pinned there. And then, as I was accepting my inevitable fate, I looked closer and saw a face. I saw *her* face. It was *Elaine.* Her eyes were burning red, but everything else was hers. She floated over me, holding me down against the mattress as she stared deeply into my eyes, spitting and snarling as she cackled. As all the tiny hairs across my body stood on end, she moved closer and began to speak.

"Oh, the look on your face!" she exclaimed with her maniacal laugh. I was still frozen as she continued. "You must be just swirling with all those nasty hows and whats and could this be real? Well the answer is of course it is silly!" If the shock on my face wasn't telling enough, the sound from the explosion of my brain was probably audible for miles. What the hell was going on?

"Well," she joyously continued, "Let's get started on this wonderful walkthrough. You see, to start things off, I must commend you. You knew that Tyler wasn't just a suicide, no matter how fried your brain was from all those recreational drugs. Proud of you." I could feel my lip twitching in anger as I tried to move myself free to no avail. She snarled and forced me farther into the bed.

"You see Cole, the thing is, we *wanted* you to find out. They saw you that night you snuck into the cemetery and we waited to see what you would do. We gave you the inside peek." This is surreal. After all this time searching, trying to find the person who killed my best friend, I had spent a night in bed with one of the people responsible. I feel like vomiting. "And if you are wondering, it was indeed me who killed your best friend." She was smiling from ear to ear at my expense. "I led him to the gates of hell and had him mutilated. Yes, Ty's body made for great ritual masses, piece by piece. The young ones are always more appealing to the prince."

"You bitch!" The words that sputtered out of my mouth shocked me. Not so much the content, but rather the fact that I could actually speak.

"Oh, feisty! But what's your next move, Cole? Are you gonna try to kill me? Well, if you do, just remember, you have to watch out for everything." A sincere look had washed over her face as she stared at me for a minute in silence. Then with a smirk, she continued, "Especially watch out for those black cats, an old friend tells me they can be just deadly." My heart stopped

as she spoke. I could feel myself sinking further and further into

the bed as my body began to shake. I remembered back to the day

I found John. I remembered just as I was walking in, I noticed a

black cat running away from the manor.

"You…" I muttered. I felt completely deflated. This

woman had taken everything from me.

"Me." She remarked, shrugging her shoulders. "You

see, it is the young ones that keep us going most definitely, but this

has always been about *you,* Cole." I somehow just kept feeling

worse and worse. That hole inside me was growing dark and deep

again. "John, well, John was just getting in the way for you. He

was standing between us, Cole. And the coven couldn't have

that."

"Why would you kill John and make it look like a

suicide?"

"Easy 20 questions, you will find everything out in

time." There was a slight pause before she continued, "The little

love note I wrote, it is true by the way. Just a sneak peek, but nonetheless true." Wow John really was my father. Every emotion I was feeling began to mix together and boil. Suddenly, I could move my arms again and I grabbed her as hard as I could and pulled her close.

"Listen to me, Elaine. I swear to God if it's the last thing I do I will kill you for this. For all of it. I'm gonna watch the light fade out of your eyes." I could see fear coming out of hiding from behind the laughing and intimidating. I could feel her starting pull away from my grip.

"You do that, Cole." She muttered as she plastered on a fake smirk and leaned in close one last time to continue, "Just remember, this isn't just me. And when you are ready to act like John Wayne, The coven will be waiting to feast on your flesh and devote you to the Lord of Darkness." And just as quick as it had happened, she shifted back into a black shadow and drifted out of the apartment, leaving me alone.

I just want to lay on this bed forever. What was I supposed to think now? Knowing who killed Ty wasn't healing at all, especially after I had just slept with her. And my father, whom

I had no memories of at all, Trained me for months to kill this girl; this *witch*, and then committed suicide and left me on my own again. Instead of killing someone, what did I do? I ran. And not only that, I ran right into the arms of the woman who I should've been hunting down. And on top of it all, turns out my father didn't actually kill himself, but she got him as well. And it was all because of me. She said that. My best and basically only friend and my own father slain because of *me.* I thought I was in a dark place before, but it doesn't get any darker than where I am now. As far as I'm concerned, the world is over. I'm done with this. I want to be done with it all.

Two days have passed and the farthest I've made it out of this supposed apartment was a few blocks to find some self-medication. That's typical of me, I guess. Every time things get hard, I blur the lines and cloak myself inside my mind. It doesn't help though. Not like I think it should. The only thing they do is turn this room into a prison and enhance the fact that I feel sorry for myself. But nonetheless, I still take them. Anything I can get my hands on, I take it and take it because it's more than feeling sorry for myself. *I am sorry.* I'm a sorry excuse for a friend. A sorry excuse for a son. And I damn sure was a sorry excuse for some bullshit vigilante hero I had been setting out to become. The world would be better off if I wasn't in it.

Hours pass; another pill. The light in the room was harsh and my vision faded. My hands began to shake vigorously and anger washed over my body. I reached for the bottle of Jameson sitting on the night stand and started chugging. I thought about Ty. All the shit we had been through together. The lifestyle we found together. The drugs, the parties, and the girls. Maybe if I had been a better role model I could have prevented him from this. Ty met Elaine through me. I thought about John as well. I spent my whole life wondering who my father was. Why he left. When I asked my mother, she looked almost frightened at the notion of talking about him and immediately brushed it off. At his mention, my grandfather always had a look of distain, and just told me I shouldn't worry about him because he was gone for good. John took me in. He helped me, even when everyone thought I was crazy, hell even I thought I was crazy. But he knew. He knew

I was right about Ty. He led me in the right direction, gave me answers, and showed me how to track the coven and extract my revenge. He was flawless in that endeavor, but I wasn't. I was sloppy. My slop led to his death.

I grabbed another pill and threw it down the hatch with another long chug of whiskey. I noticed my knife in its sheath on the opposite nightstand. Thoughts of my screw ups raced through my mind as I took another swig. I launched that bottle of Jameson, and it slammed into the wall, shattering into a million pieces. A tear rolled down my cheek as I took a step towards the nightstand. Suddenly, the room was chilled by a cold air, and a whisper caught my ear. I stopped, somewhat expecting now to see something sinister pop up again. I braced myself as the voice broke through clearer. It was familiar. Then, I saw him appear. He was transparent, but he was here, standing right in front of me. It was Ty.

"Hey, bitch. You crying?" The voice sent chills down my spine. I must have drank more than even I could handle, although that is definitely something he would say. "What's the matter Cole, cat got your tongue?"

"Is that some kind of joke?" I can't believe I was responding to this-well whatever it was.

"I thought it was funny."

"Ty, is this really you?"

"It's me."

"Why are you here? How are you here?"

"Why are *you* still here, Cole? I mean seriously, you're thinking about killing yourself?" I lowered my head at that statement. The thought of suicide sounded so much more ridiculous out loud. "I mean it man, that's not the kid I know. Cole, where's the mother fucker that held me up after my father got put in jail for beating my mother almost to death? Where's the kid who was a big brother, a father to me my whole life?"

"It's not like that man."

"It isn't? Cole you were always the strongest kid I knew. You always stood up for people. Sure you had your faults, we both did. But you never let anyone get punked. You were always a good kid man, you were just scared of it."

"Ty, you're gone man." I wiped away tears from my eyes. "This isn't fighting a school bully or helping a friend. You died. My father was killed. There's a coven of witches sacrificing to the devil in our woods and I just slept with the ringleader. I *can't* handle it."

"Yes you can. I know more than you can imagine now that I've passed." Ty was filled with as much fire as I could remember.

"What do you mean?"

"Me, and your dad, your mother, all of it was meant to happen."

"my *mother?* What the hell are you talking about?"

"Listen Cole, this thing, it's bigger than you know. There's a lot John didn't tell you and that bitch only teased you with the surface of it in that bogus letter. That's why I'm here. I found my way back so I could tell you." What was I supposed to make of this? My whole life is tail spinning out of control. I was talking to my dead best friend for Christ's sake.

"What do you have to tell me then, Ty? What don't I know?"

"Well first off, she was telling you the truth when she said this is all about you."

"Thank you that really helps, now I'm gonna save the day."

"You need to hear this, Cole. What you need to realize next is that she is not Elaine; at least not anymore."

"What?" I muttered in shock.

"That was a big player, maybe the biggest of all. Her name is Lilith, I think John may have clued you in on her." I remembered back on my time at the manor. Lilith was the first. The lover of Lucifer and matriarch of the witches. My spine shivered.

"Yeah I Remember her."

"This whole time she's been trying to break you."

"It's working," I stated with a smile.

"The coven, they don't just do spells or worship the devil, but they worship *all* devils."

"All devils?"

"Yeah. Demons, the ones who fell with Lucifer. There are very powerful ones, and Lilith is Lucifer's favorite."

"So Elaine is Lilith?"

"No, not entirely. Elaine is her physical representation. The fact that Lilith has taken over means Elaine has been dead for some time."

"This is crazy, man."

"Crazy is relative asshole, you're talking to a ghost." The irony of this whole conversation hit me. He was right. I decided to shut up and listen. "Listen, what they want to do is get Lilith and Lucifer on Earth. That is the goal of this coven. The reason it revolves around you is there's a catch to getting Lucifer and Lilith free."

"What's that?"

"Brothers. One born evil. One committing to the most mortal sin of all."

"What does that have to do with me?"

"Don't you get it man? What was considered the most mortal sin back in the day?"

"I don't know, suicide?"

"Exactly. Don't you see? She was pushing you there, and it almost worked. Me, your father, having sex with you it was all a work to get you to kill yourself."

"But what about the other part? I don't have a brother."

"How do you know for sure?"

"My mother never mentioned one, and neither did my grandfather after she passed."

"Your mother didn't mention a lot of things."

"What the fuck does that mean?"

"Your mother was a witch, Cole. I know you don't want to hear that but it's true."

"Jesus, Ty I don't know how much more of this shit I can handle. Even when you're dead you're an ass."

"I mean it dude. That's why John went away for so long. He knew what I'm telling you now. When he found out, he told her father, and left with the church, but it was too late. She was already pregnant. He learned how to hunt witches with the church and saved many towns doing so. Until he came back to save you."

"This, this is just too much…"

"If you don't believe me man, do this town a favor and go back."

"Back where? I don't have anywhere to go!"

"Go back to John's, Cole. Everything you need to know is there."

"Then what, huh?"

"Then, you go be a goddamn hero. You have to be." Ty vanished with a flicker of the light. My head was spinning. *Was my mother really a witch? Was I really even seeing Ty?* I mean for all my self medication, this could all be in my head. But the other night, that *was* real—whether I wanted it to be or not. Despite it all, Ty was right. I needed to go back. I don't know if I can be the hero he wants, but I need to go back, and connect all the dots. Tonight I'm going back to Eden.

The trip in the Camaro was as short as it was frightening. I pulled into the driveway of John's manor and I almost lost it. The memory of everything hit me like a ton of bricks. My hair stood on end as I got out of the car and stood there, staring at the old house. All I could picture was seeing John hanging there when I walked in. The thought scared me to death. I could feel myself about to vomit.

I finally mustered up the courage to walk in, all be it shaking the entire way. I headed straight into the study, which was trashed the same as it was when I left it. I walked around looking, trying to decipher where the information was that I would be looking for. I saw the book of The Old Religion, and I remembered reading it with John. Under it were a few old books on different ways to fight off things that go bump in the night, including demons. It was clear I was about to have a long night catching up.

After reading book after book and sorting through the immense papers lying around, I learned two things: John was a badass, and Ty, well he was right. Everything he said was true. John came back to save me after my grandfather died, because he was the one protecting me from the coven. And it turns out that my mother wasn't a cancer victim, but some other members of the church who did what John did got to her first. My grandfather stayed back with my mother despite her being a witch because of me. He was there to make sure she couldn't hurt me. What I don't get, and judging by his journals what John didn't get, is where the other brother came in. John was closing in before his death, but had no solid leads.

It was all there, sitting on an old mahogany desk right in front of my face. I still couldn't convince myself to do anything with it. What was I supposed to do with it? It was different with John behind me. I'm just a kid. Just a teenager with an attitude and a drug problem. *I am not a hero.* I can't be. I'm not good enough. I am not John.

As I sat here mulling over everything that I had read, my phone rang. November Rain sounded sweetly from my pocket. It was Katie. I hit ignore and wondered what she could possibly want the way things ended the last time we talked. I shook my head and continued to waver on what I should do next.

The next few hours went by slow, as I spent it pacing back and forth between the house and the car and the out building where I left my Harley. I was at the trunk of the Camaro, staring at my hickory axe when a set of headlights turned into the drive. At first, I gripped the axe and began to pull it all the way out of the trunk until I saw what kind of car it was. It was a white prius. It was Katie. I walked over towards the prius to meet her. Her Auburn hair flowed in the slight breeze as she stepped out; she was an angel in a REO Speedwagon shirt, faded flare jeans and flip flops. She looked scared as she stepped towards me to start talking.

"Where have you been, Cole?"

"I didn't think you would be concerned with where I was, Katie." I was still trying to figure out what she was wanting to see me for. Whatever it was, it seems serious.

"Cole something huge is going down here. I think you might have been right about what you said before you left."

"What's happened? And how did you even know where this place was?"

"You aren't the only one who knows how to find things, Cole." That was so like her. Always with the witty response.

"Right...back to the pressing matter, what the hell happened? You look like you've seen a ghost."

"Three more kids have gone missing at school. The same way as all the others. Not as sloppy as Ty, but still brushed off by the police. And I had something very weird happen working a shift at the pub."

"What was it?"

"That group of men were back, and they hit on me, like they did that day while they were in the bar. But the weird part was Elaine was with them." I could feel my blood boiling at the mention of her name.

"Did they try anything when you left?"

"They just watched me leave. It was weird. She was weird."

"Listen to me Katie, I was right. It's about the kids, and it's about me. I can't really explain but you need to stay as far away from Elaine as you can. She is dangerous."

"Okay. Cole, what are you going to do?"

"I don't know. What can I do? I can't stop them, not without John."

"That's such a load of shit, Cole!" The way she was looking at me I thought I was in for a smack. I swear it's like walking on eggshells around this girl, I honestly don't even know what I said wrong this time.

"What's a load of shit? And why is it that every time I see you it's a shouting match?"

"It's a load of shit that you think you aren't good enough for *anything!* You are always selling yourself short no matter what we are talking about and I don't know why."

"What do you expect from me, Katie? I'm just a kid. We are just kids. You're talking about taking on an entire coven of witches in the woods who spend their time worshiping the freaking devil himself."

"So what, Cole? Your best friend dies, you lose the reins on the insane life you lead and eventually leave town with some stranger for months to learn everything you can about some fairytale story about witches. Then after all that time and effort, and everything you found out, you're just gonna walk away and ignore it? That's not you."

"Katie, I'm nobody's hero. I can't do it. I *can't.*"

"You're mine." Two words have never come closer to knocking me off my feet in my life. As a matter of fact, I don't recall anything hitting me that hard, and Blake has given it a few shots over the years. I was stunned.

"I appreciate the inspiration, but pitty isn't gonna help."

"I mean it, Cole. You are my hero. You always have been. You have been through so much in your life already; you never had time to be a kid. You have always been years ahead of the rest of us, that's what made you so attractive. But you have taken everything that has happened in stride. I have never seen you complain about any of it. And not to mention if anyone I know is brave, it's you. You spent your entire schooling career standing up for kids you didn't even know so that bullies like Blake couldn't ruin their days. Nobody else will even make eye contact with him, and you've put him in his place hundreds of times without hesitation. The Cole Harris that I know is fearless. He's a little bit reckless, but smart, strong, and an exceptional adjuster. He was born to be a hero; not just mine, but just maybe this entire towns."

Those two simple words before were almost enough to knock me down, but they paled in comparison to what I just heard her say. Very few times in my life have I ever been speechless, but twice within minutes she's brought me there. I stood there, frozen in thought…could she be right? Is that really *me?* What am I supposed to say to that? I did my best to collect myself before responding.

"Katie; I'm scared." Not exactly the way I was wanting to go but the truth just blurted out of me faster than my mind could stop it. "I'm not this fearless guy that you remember. I'm broken; they've broken me. Even if I want to go after them, I don't see a way out, and I'm scared as hell."

"Cole, being fearless doesn't mean you're never afraid. It's having the ability to admit your fear and then facing it head on anyways. You've always done that with so much confidence. You can do it now. I know you're scared, you've admitted it. Now go and face it. Be the man that I'm in love with and save the place we call home."

"What was that?"

"Cole, I love you. Sometimes I try to hide it and for a while I was trying to bury it because you were in such a dark place but I've always loved you."

"Wow. I don't know how much more of this I can take." I was shaking all over. It seems like around every turn lately I have ran into intense news like this. The only difference here is that I have been waiting to hear those words since we split up. This was *great* news.

"Cole, the reason I can tell you now is I can see the light in you. You're still in a dark place, but there's a light. But you *have* to use it. You have to stop these people."

"Katie, I love you too. And you're right, I need to stop them. I'm just afraid."

"Cole I need to go, but you need to find something inside of you to stand up and fight. I need you to. Everyone needs you to." She grabbed my face and kissed my cheek before climbing back into her car and leaving. She left me standing there blankly like so many times before, but this time I was happy. Happier than I have been in years.

I spent the rest of the night cleaning the manor and thinking about Katie and what she said while I got ready to sleep. Just the thought of being able to sleep again was almost surreal. I laid down in the same upstairs bed I spent all those nights in after learning from john all day. As I took off my dog tags, kissing them like usual, I let a small yet long overdue smile break through as I sat them on the nightstand.

The sound of November Rain once again hits my ears. Katie. What could she want? What *time* was it? I reach for my phone. Katie's beautiful face lights up the screen. The time says three o clock. It was odd for her to be up so late and calling, but after today, I had no idea what to really expect from her. I woke myself up enough to be coherent before answering. Then, with a slide to unlock, I heard her voice.

"Hiya, honey! You never called!" Elaine's voice invaded my body, sending chills down my spine. Fear and intense rage simultaneously washed over me.

"What the hell are you doing with her phone?"

"What? No hello?"

"Just tell me where she is or so help me God…"

"What? Is that supposed to scare me? What *exactly* are you and your God gonna do, Cole?"

"Well, He might just turn His head, but I'll start by slitting your fucking throat just slow enough to make you choke down your own blood before the light fades from your eyes, bitch."

"Easy, tiger. Wouldn't want you to get too excited…again." She laughed at her sick joke as I began to fill with hatred. "I'll tell you where she is." I'm ready to kill her. I swear if Katie is hurt it will be the end of everything in this town that even resembles evil. "Cole," she continued, "If you want to see your little crush untouched and alive, come to the woods tomorrow during the witching hour. We will have her there and I'm sure we can work out some kind of a deal. See you soon lover!"

My blood was boiling out of my skin. I launched my phone into the hardwood floor, shattering it into a million pieces. I spent about ten or fifteen minutes pacing around the room wandering what just happened and what I should do. It was no doubt a trap. Katie may not even be alive. But I sat down on the bed and thought about something she had said earlier about finding something inside of me to stand up to the coven and fight. Well I think Elaine just helped me find it. And for her sake and anyone who stands between me and her, they better hope Katie is okay, because witches or not, they haven't seen hell like I was about to unleash. It was on. It's time for me to end it all. Tomorrow night, I single handedly kill this coven.

If You Want Blood...You Got It

Seven A.M. Four hours passed by slower than the old lady looking for a handicapped spot at Kroger. I spent a lot of those first couple hours sulking, getting back to how I felt that night I found out about Elaine. Self pitty and depression began to seep through the pours of my skin inward into my soul. Then I started thinking about Ty and Katie. Not just feeling sorry for their situations but actually thinking about *them.* I thought about how hard they fought to get me to do the right thing here. Ty literally defied death to open my eyes and keep me alive. And Katie, she believes in me, even when nobody else does including myself. I've done nothing to deserve that, especially from her. But I'm slowly beginning to realize, I've also done nothing to deserve all of the shit this coven has caused either.

After my epiphany, I've been spending the rest of my time up until now going over my Harley and other things, namely my axe. I went over her beautiful hickory handle I made for it after I found the mauler at my grandpa's property. The subtle stain I used when refinishing it complimented the grain beautifully. I ran my hands over the wood up to the mauler I modified into a double edge witch-killing machine. The blades on either end came out a little uneven, but very good for a first time edge maker. And boy were they sharp. Sharp enough to shave a lumberjack's beard. But I don't need to shave a beard, I need a one hitter, clean cut slice, witch decapitating axe. I remembered I always kept a whetstone in the leather bag of my Harley for my knives. Sharpening my creation would be a good way to free my mind and refocus to the task at hand: killing some witches.

After soaking the stone for about 20 minutes, I was satisfied. I sat it out on a workbench in the garage and positioned my axe over the stone. Tilting the first side of the blade at a slight angle, I began to gently slide it back towards me; curving with the direction of the blade. Back and forth I drug, carful not to dig into the stone. When I was happy with that side, then came the other. The sound of the metal scraping against the stone soothed me. It was serene. I repeated these steps on the other end of my double

bladed decapitator, ensuring a razor sharp finish to either side. I

was focused; happy. The worries had subsided at least for now. I

decided to keep the good vibes going by sharpening my bowie

knife.

As I slid the blade back and forth on the stone, I

thought about just what the knife meant to me. My grandfather

gave it to me as a gift before my first hunt. I was so nervous that

day I could barely hold up the gun. Through the hours of waiting,

my excitement never waivered. I couldn't believe my grandpa was

passing on one of his passions to me. Then finally, out from the

brush stepped a massive 12 point buck grazing in a hay field. With

a reassuring nod from Grandpa, I raised his 12 gauge, and as the

buck raised his head, I pulled the trigger and dropped him flat.

Grandpa was so pleased with me after my first hunt that not only

did we use this knife to clean the deer, but we took one of his tines

and made the bone handle it has today. I've carried it with me

every day since then, it's become like a family member to me.

And tonight this family member will be on my hip, ready to decapitate witches and exact revenge.

It was going to take more than a couple sharp blades for one man to dispel a coven of witches by himself, no matter how much Katie believed in me. So I starting making my plan. The basis of this plan is pretty simple: fight fire with fire. I remembered what I had read on the old time witch-hunts and what I learned from John about witches and burning at the stake. But this was bigger than using a single shot flare gun or homemade bomb. It was more personal than that. The sun was almost all the way up in the sky now as I set out on my way to put forth my plan to even the score.

I stepped off the Harley and put the kickstand out as I started making my way towards the cemetery. Walking over to the equipment shed I could tell Fergus, the graves keeper, wasn't here today. Fergus was an old friend of my grandfather's, and he had run the graveyard for as long as I could remember. I was building my plan around access to Fergus' backhoe, so the fact that he wasn't here just made it all that much easier. I stepped away from the shed for a minute however, to get an idea of where my next move would take place. I'm pretty sure there's no danger of running into any hags or flying bitches in the daylight, but just in case, my knife was at my side.

I walked through the beginnings of the woods, remembering when I ran through them just a short while ago, fearing for my life. Now I was here, walking into it all. As I walked, I found a good spot to act out what was in my mind. There was a U shaped trail that encroached about 100 yards into the woods adjacent to the equipment shed where Fergus had kept his extra fill dirt for the graves. Several of the brush trails that led deeper into the woods dumped at or near this little clearing. It was perfect. Now I just needed to do a little 'borrowing' from the shed.

I walked back over to the shed, and the door was locked. Luckily for me, the spare key was on the door ledge, just like every other place in this small town. I opened the door and walked in. It sat there in between an old beat down dump truck and a few mowers. A rusty yellow CAT. I grinned as I walked over to the overhang garage door and pulled it up and open. The morning sun shone in, lighting up the contents of the shed. I

stepped up into the Backhoe and turned the key to start it up. The

diesel engine rumbled and grumbled, but after a few minutes it was

warmed up and ready to go. I putt putted my way over to my U

trail and followed it back into the woods. I drove the backhoe into

the middle of the trail's curve and turned it so the back would face

the clearing inside the 'U'. The engine idled triumphantly as I

pushed the levers for the stabilizers forward, setting them to the

ground. Scoop after scoop I dug deeper, curling the bucket as I

pulled up and out to dump the dirt over with Fergus' excess fill

dirt. Once the hole was about 12 feet deep and 16 feet wide, I was

satisfied.

      After I placed the backhoe back in the shed and locked

everything up the way I found it, I rode the Harley back to the U

trail and used my axe to cut down some dead branches and fallen

logs in the woods. Once I had a hefty enough pile, I pushed it into

the hole and climbed in. I took 8 thicker diameter logs and stuck

them into the ground in the corners, just to stabilize everything. I

widdled the tops of the rest of the branches to a point, sticking the smaller ones alone in the ground, and the taller ones in the center, all stuck sharp side up. I stepped up onto the corner logs and lifted myself out, careful not to fall back on the stickers. I looked back at it, happy with what I had made. I covered the top with leafy branches that had fallen to hide my work. Once I got them in there, it was a matter of burning the bunch of them as they lay impaled in their grave.

It was about noon now, and my stomach was roaring. I decided to head back into town for the first time since I had been at the school to get some lunch. I slowed down once I got to grandpa's land and turned in. I partly pulled in due to shock at the overgrowth, but it was mostly because Elaine's uncle had put a for sale sign up in the driveway. I hopped off my Harley and took in the unfamiliar sights of weeds and overgrown grass and shrubs. The only clear part was the new paved driveway Kevin must have had put in. I can't believe that bastard just went under me like that. He has always wanted this land, even when grandpa was alive. The thing was, despite the weeds, it was empty. There was no cabin, no garage, the pond was disgusting, and the driveway was paved. Grandpa wasn't here anymore. He was with me. Nevertheless, I kicked the sign down into the weeds, just to spite the greedy prick.

I drove on, hitting town in no time. Nothing was different to the eye about Eden, but the aura over the town was chilling. I wasn't sure who was going to be a witch. My eyes had been opened to my 'innocent' little small town. The pub was bustling as usual as I pulled into the parking lot. Upon walking in, I noticed the usual characters, Addison's little posse of ass kissers. Kevin Walker was the biggest of them all, and there he was. I had half a mind to trot over to the smug son of a bitch and knock his block off for moving in on my grandfather's land like he did, but I just stared him down as I picked a bar stool and motioned for a drink.

"You oughtta know that fake ID don't work around here, son. Eden isn't a big enough town for me not to know who you are." Addison Miller himself said to me as he looked me over with a stark intensity.

"Yeah you oughtta know just about how big this shit hole town is considering half of it is stuck up your ass." He smirked disapprovingly at the sarcastic remark.

"You know Cole, it's remarks like that that could end up getting you in trouble one day." He was glaring at me as he handed me a soda. I could feel his eyes trying to burn through me. I looked to my right down the end of the bar and all of his goonies were giving me the same twilight zone stare.

"Maybe that day's today, huh Addison?" he shrugged as he looked over at Kevin and the others and began to laugh hysterically. I pushed the drink back towards him and stood to leave.

"Hey, Kevin. Thanks for putting a for sale sign on grandpa's land by the way. Always knew Elaine was a cock sucker but now I know it runs in the family."

"YOU HAVE NO IDEA WHO YOU'RE MOUTHING OFF TO BOY!" He shouted as he tried to run at me and the rest of his minion buddies held him back. I smiled as he rustled around for a few seconds before calming back down. Then I turned towards the door, nodding at Addison as I walked back out.

As I walked across the parking lot to my Harley, I noticed something had been placed on it. Not knowing what exactly this thing was that was sitting on the seat of my Harley, I proceeded cautiously with my hand close to my knife.

The closer I came to the Harley, the more apparent it was. The shimmer of the scales, and the round layers of coils gave it away. There was a snake on my bike. A freaking python there, staring me in the face. I was standing there, trying to figure out how to proceed moving this snake from my seat so I could leave, and I heard a voice. It came from somewhere behind me, floating over my shoulder and into my ear.

"That's an omen, you know." The voice was a familiar one. I thought back to where I had heard it before, and then it hit me. It was the voice from the library. The first time I met John. It was Mrs. Winfred's voice. She stepped out from her place behind me and walked over to the snake, picking it up and holding it as she continued. "He's an omen," she said. "He's here to make a statement to you. Serpents are a sign of evil; a symbol for the devil himself." She ran her hands across the snake comforting it as she talked. She was staring at me intensely.

"I've read the books, lady." I was already more than irritated by this point, and I was starting to get the obvious hint that every damn person in this town is a part of this coven. I was alone in my quest for revenge.

"I'm sure you have, dear. John spared not a detail with you; I'd take that to the bank." How did she know that? The thought of someone like her talking about John didn't sit well with me either way. "John wasn't a lone warrior against this coven, you know…" she said as she smirked at me. *What the hell was she talking about?* She read the look of confusion on my face and continued, "That means neither are you, dear. This is your battle, I understand, but there is a network of people that are here to help win the war. You will find out what I mean soon enough." I nodded in fear as she took the snake and walked away. *What network was she talking about? The church? Were there more people like John—like me out there?* I saddled my motorcycle as I tried to juggle all the questions in my mind. One thing was for

sure though; it was time. Time to drive into hell and change my

life forever.

If You Want Blood…You Got It Part II

The sun was setting now. I looked out at the ominous evening sky from John's porch, wondering what I was getting myself into. As doubt began to creep into my mind, the words that Katie had said to me washed over me. "You're my hero," she said. And the more that I look back on it, she was right. Sometimes I try to deny it; sometimes I want to run away from it. As much as I may not want the responsibility, it was true. I was the guy. I *have* to go against this coven. This is bigger than me and my doubts; it's about an entire town. It's about my father. It's about the girl that I love.

I strapped my axe across my back and holstered a flare gun at my side. With a deep breath of night air, I had done everything I could to prepare myself for the Armageddon that lie ahead. With Katie on my mind and in my heart, I started my Harley and rode off towards the cemetery.

The cold night air sliced through my body as I rode up the old mine road to the back of the cemetery. I pulled up and shut off my motorcycle beside Fergus' equipment shed. The wind whipped sounds from deep in the forest out towards me. Shrieks and moans filled my ears, and the smell of incense filled my nostrils. I clutched my flare gun in my left hand as I began to proceed. As I approached a small entrance trail, sets of eyes danced across the brush farther into the woods. Suddenly, the stench of rotten eggs filled the air. I stopped, and in the gateway of the trail entrance Elaine appeared. She wore a white gown which scantily lay across her body, exposing almost as much as it concealed. She was barefoot and extremely light on the ground; almost as if she was floating. Her eyes were pure white as if they had rolled into the back of her head. With her arms outstretched, she cocked her head back and let out an otherworldly cackle, shaking the ground beneath me.

"Howdy lover!" she professed with disgusting joy. "Glad to see you made it. Our girl must have really pulled on those heartstrings huh?" Hearing her talk about Katie was lighting a fire inside of me, but I was frozen. Something about Elaine seemed different. She seemed bigger, more ominous.

"I didn't come for small talk, Elaine. Just tell me where she is and we can all walk away from this." She screeched in laughter mocking me as she levitated higher into the sky.

"Isn't it clear to you yet Cole? There is no walking away from this. Not for you, nor for Elaine, just the same as Tyler and Katie couldn't walk away."

"Yeah…you're probably right. It was worth a shot though. I'm going to give you one last chance though."

"Really?! *You're* going to give *me* one final chance?" Again she cackled loudly as she continued to rise into the dark sky above. She was about ten or more feet in the air now. Fear is creeping into my body. But she can't know that. *I'm a hero.*

"That's right, sweetheart. All you have to do is take me to Katie. Just show her to me and I won't kill you right now." My palms were sweating profusely. I kept my hand steady on the flare gun as I watched her intently.

"Alright, Cole. You talked me into it." I stood there perplexed, unable to speak. "What's the matter Cole, not the answer you expected?" I shrugged my shoulders in a 'what do you expect' kind of agreement. She began to float down and the night got eerily quiet. Her eyes rolled forward as she touched the ground and turned a fiery red. She grinned at me, and then continued, "Well, you aren't as dopey as they say lover." My eyes widened and hair stood on end as I wondered what she meant. "It's never that easy with me, sugar. Oh Cole, you were so close. You thought you would just ride in here like John Wayne and shoot at a few witches and call it a night? Preposterous. This little town is just a dot on the map of a much bigger scale, honey. And I'm no witch. I'm Lilith, the mother of demons, the bride of Lucifer. I am their leader, Cole." I could hear branches snapping behind me. As I turned to my sides I could see shadows surrounding me in the darkness. I thought about pulling my flare gun, but there were more bodies than I could count. I was screwed. "Tonight," she continued, "I bring my groom back from the pit!" The red glow of her eyes lit up the night. I could see the witches who surrounded me. There were at least 20 of them. Without notice, they converged on me at once, grabbing me and walking towards the woods, following Lilith, swaying to a now present flute coming from deep in the woods.

The cloaked followers walked all around me to keep me from escaping while two brutes walked beside me, holding onto ropes that bound my wrists. Flashes of yellow glowing eyes accompanied quick rustling in the bush on either side of the trails. Laughing and moaning came from all sides. The cloaked group around me hummed in unison to the hypnotic sound of the flute ahead. Smells of rotten eggs, fire, and decomposition mixed together in the night air forming a pungent aroma that solidified the cruelty of what lie ahead.

We reached a clearing in the woods where what seemed like hundreds of witches danced around an overwhelming fire. The old hags danced joyously, causing their pale naked bodies to jiggle in the flickering light. They were all chanting something in Latin to the sound of the flute. The flute was closer now, but still seemed to be coming from deeper in the woods. The group of followers that had forced me here walked me over to a large pole that had a raised podium for me to stand on. Despite my best efforts, they lifted me up onto the podium, and tied me to the pole.

All I could do now was watch and wonder what I was thinking getting myself into all of this. *Did I really think I was going to come out on top versus all of these evil people?* Elaine, or Lilith as she was calling herself, trounced around the fire skipping happily and chanting along with the others. Suddenly, after her third trip around the fire, she stopped on a dime directly in front of me, staring at me with an unmatched hate firing the red glow of her eyes. She threw her arms out to her sides, motioning for the others to quiet down. In the silence she again began to levitate upwards, and floated over towards my podium.

"Well lover, it's time. You were too stupid to just kill yourself like we needed you to. Now I guess I have to move on to plan B." I was about twenty feet off of the ground and this *thing* posing as Elaine was floating in the air, glaring at me eye to eye.

"What's plan B?" I said with a smirk. I was just trying to stall as long as I could now. *How in the hell was I going to get out of this?*

"Oh honey, there's multiple avenues to the end game. And unfortunately for you, we don't need you around for the other avenues. We have got what we need out of you." She smiled and winked at me like that statement was supposed to mean something to me.

"Hold on, sugar. I want you to humor me for a minute." She grinned wildly at the pet name I had given her and gave me a look of affirmation.

"Well, I guess I could, but why should I?"

"Hey, I'm dying anyway." I said as I shrugged. "Just answer a few quick questions for me is all I'm asking."

"Alright, Alright. What could it hurt?" I smiled at her as she backed away from the podium and asked what I wanted to know. I began to slowly work the rope that tied my hands behind me across a sharp knot in the pole. This was my chance.

"Well, I know that John is my father and my mother was a member of this cult. But why me? Why does this all revolve around me?"

"Cole, my lover, your mother was more than just a member. Honey, she was the queen." My heart sank as I remembered my mother as a beautiful woman. *Could she really be capable of this?* "John was more than just some guy that happened to be your father, too."

"Oh really?" I did my best to persuade her to continue while I tried to cut the rope without being noticed.

"Yes, of course dear," she continued, "Your father was chosen. It was told through legend that the witch born of a righteous man will bear the son of a pure hero. And it was told that this son must be tempted into committing the ultimate sin, and his blood will open the pit and allow Lucifer to walk free."

"And that son is me, huh? See, I always told my math teacher I would turn out to be something important; too bad she can't see me now." She rolled her eyes as I asked another question. "So, who is helping you get these kids?" A prideful smile washed over her face as she moved in close to answer.

"I don't know what you're talking about." She said mockingly. "Like I said before, there are many other avenues in place, in the case that we couldn't convince you to kill yourself. We should have known you would be stubborn like your father. Anyways, I'm done with the Q&A. It's time we end this experiment, lover." *What was I going to do?* I had barely gotten a small tear in the rope by now, and she was done talking. The hair on my body began to stand as Elaine moved backwards in the air and threw her hands out to the side. The witches began to chant loudly as she threw her head back. Thunder cracked above as a storm came raging in. lighting was bouncing off her fingertips. This was it. I had failed John. I had failed Katie. I let them win. *I was going to die.*

Suddenly the coven stopped chanting and turned their attention into the woods. Something was wrong. The storm quieted and Elaine turned her attention towards the group, looking concerned. There was an eerie silence now. Then, from the cover of the woods came the loud ring of a 12 gauge shotgun. One of the witches flew back. It was a direct hit. Shrieks began to fill the woods as Elaine flew around hectically, trying to find the gunman. Shot after shot rang out as the witches fell victim one by one to buckshot. Elaine and the rest of the coven that were unhurt frantically ran into the woods to search for the shooter. There was a loud commotion from inside the cover of the trees, and then someone emerged with a shotgun running towards me...it was Blake.

"What the hell are you doing here Blake?" I shouted as he ran towards the podium to help get me down.

"These guys came after me and kidnapped me about a week ago. I had just got out of the hospital after our run in and I thought I was going to meet up with Damien and hang out."

"Damien? I found his class ring out here not too long ago, I thought he was one of the missing." I was in shock as Blake cut my hands free and we got down to my axe and flare gun.

"No Cole, Damien is the one leading kids to this group of crazies. They were going to kill me. The only thing that saved me is they wanted you to think I was in on it, so they tortured me and eventually let me go. I came back tonight to get some revenge and saw you getting tied up."

I couldn't believe Blake's story. I almost felt bad for the way I had treated him. He was the *last* person I thought would be saving me. In any event, we were on borrowed time. The witches were screaming back towards us through the woods, being led by Elaine.

"Blake, listen to me. I'm sure you've gathered these aren't normal people we are dealing with. Those naked ladies are witches and the floating girl from our high school is actually a demon. Don't ask questions. If you use that shot gun, aim for the witches heads. Here's a flare gun. Fire is better. Just follow me and hopefully we will make it out of this alive."

We took off towards the woods in the direction of my pit, but we were too slow. The witches were surrounding us, waiting to pick us off as we entered the woods. Their eyes glowed inside the tree line. Thunder cracked loud again. Elaine was back. An ear piercing screech filled the air as she flew up above us.

"Go Cole! Get the hell out of here!" Blake yelled at me as Elaine stalked us from the sky.

"What are you gonna do Blake? I'm not leaving you here with a hundred witches."

"You won't be. I"ll hold off Elaine, you lead the witches to whatever your plan was. I trust you. You're more important to this than me." This was so weird. Blake seemed completely changed. *I couldn't just leave a guy there could I?* There was no time. The witches were slowly starting to close in. Elaine wasn't going to wait up there forever. I had to go. I looked at Blake, nodded and grabbed my axe.

"Hey, Golden Girls!" I shouted as I ran towards the trail to my pit, "Come catch me. I want you to tie me up again!" I took off down the trail and could hear them following me. Leaves and branches rustled behind me as I could hear the herd tromping behind me. I weaved in and out of the trails. I was going down random trails and circling back so that they wouldn't catch on. I could hear faint screams of Blake far off behind me. I felt terrible for leaving him behind.

I'm coming up on the pit now. I sped up a little to create distance and get around the pit. The witches broke through the clearing and stared at me like a wolf staring at a juicy t bone.

"Hey girls." I shouted at them. They began to cautiously walk towards me smiling and cackling along the way. "I hope y'all didn't mind that golden girls comment," I continued, "No hard feelings on my end. Anyhow, I gotta get out of these woods now. Can't let y'all kill me. Sorry ladies." I waved and Jetted away down the trail towards the cemetery keepers shed. The coven let out a communal scream as they blitzed the trail to catch up to me.

I took a side trail and circled back to watch the inevitable. As the first wave made it to the pit, they fell through and hit the sticks with massive force, impaling themselves all the way through. Their screeches and cries pierced the night air. The secondary part of the group tried to stop in time but the back end ran into the ones in front, knocking them in and entrapping them. I stepped out axe in hand, and smiled at the few who remained. They snarled at me and ran in my direction. I met them halfway and with a swift swing, I decapitated the first one clean. As the next one came in, I spun and delivered the blade of my axe to her stomach, spilling her end trails onto the forest floor. The last one tried to run away, so I chased her down, jumping on her back and slicing her neck to the bone with my knife. I dragged her back and threw the remaining three in the pit. I dug out the gas can I had stashed next to the pit and dumped it on them. Moans and weeping grew loud as they knew their demise were near. I lit a match and with the flick of my wrist, wiped out all of Elaine's minions.

Amidst the painful cries of the witches burning in the pit, my attention turned back towards where I had just ran from. Blake. *Was he okay?* I never thought I would be asking myself such a question, but there's a lot of new things now that I never could have dreamt of. I began my way quickly back through the trails towards the clearing I had escaped, leaving behind me a pit full of half dead witches and the smell of human flesh burning. As I weaved through the woods, I could hear cries for help. It was Blake. I was running now. Branches smacked against me unforgivingly as I picked up speed to reach the clearing. I was getting closer, but the cries were growing quieter by the second. Sprinting my way through one last turn, I reached the opening, and what I saw stopped me dead in my tracks.

Blake was lying there, face battered and his torso torn apart. He was using one hand to push himself up against a log so he could sit up and the other hand to hold his innards in. I walked over to him slowly in disbelief. He was crying, and spitting up his own blood. A look of fear and disappointment took over his face as he saw me.

"Blake? What the hell happened, man?" I knew that question was pretty much self explanatory but I was in shock and didn't know what else to say.

"I tried to run like you told me to, Cole. The witches all followed you and I ran as hard as I could to the tree line. But it was too late. Elaine was there waiting on me."

"Elaine did this?" I bent down and tried to pull his hand back so I could see exactly what the damage was.

"Cole, no!" Blake shouted at me as he gurgled on blood. A piece of his intestine slipped out some from where I had moved his hand. His skin was ivory white and ice cold to the touch.

"Blake, I'm sorry man. I don't know what to do." His eyes were scanning franticly. I could tell this was it.

"Cole, did it work? How did you get away? Did I do good, Cole?" he coughed again and black blood came out from deep inside him.

"Blake, you did real good. Because of you, I was able to get the witches." He looked at me and forced a half smile. "I set their asses on fire." His smile quickly faded as he coughed hard two more times, spilling more of his contents. He began to shake vigorously.

"Cole, you gotta help me." He was grabbing on to me, pleading.

"Blake, you know there isn't anything I can do. I wish there was." I wiped a tear away as he began to slip further into death.

"Cole please, do something for me. I don't want to go like this. I'm scared. It hurts Cole, it hurts." I looked away to stop myself from crying. The one time this kid decided to be decent it cost him his life. I saw his shotgun sitting off to the side in the tall grass. I looked back at Blake's pale face and knew I had to do it. It was going to be brutal and nasty, but God help me I had to do it.

I got up from Blake and walked over to his shotgun. I picked it up and pumped it once to load the chamber. I walked back over to Blake, who was mumbling something and slipping in and out of consciousness. Tears began to roll down my cheeks as I pulled the gun up to my shoulder.

"Blake, I'm real sorry it has to be this way. I really am. But this is all that I can do for you. Just know, you did a good job. I'm proud of you. You were a hero tonight." Blake was looking off into the sky. I'm not sure if he understood me or not. I tightened my grip on the gun, and pointed the barrel towards his head. I was breathing heavy, trying to keep composure. I took one last breath in, closed my eyes, and pulled the trigger. With one loud bang, Blake and his pain were gone. He was gone because of me. I wiped his blood off of my face and left his body there, torso torn apart and face half blown off, lying in a pool of his own blood. I had to go find Elaine. I have to stop all this. I *am* stopping all this. It ends *tonight*.

I made my way across the clearing and past the big fire looking for Elaine. There were noises coming from deeper in the woods, it sounded like more chanting, and the distant playing of a flute. *That's* where I needed to go.

"Elaine!" I shouted as I made my way slowly through the woods. "Where are you, you stupid bitch?" I know that She is going to try to surprise me, so I was trying to draw her out. "Come on, you just had me! Don't tell me you're afraid now!" Suddenly I could hear her wretched cackling from the woods around me. She was here now. It was time.

"Hiya, Sugar!" I could hear her voice coming from what seemed like several directions around me. "I couldn't find you earlier, so I had to settle for another one of your classmates."

"I saw your handywork. Only the toughest Demon girls go after an ignorant kid who they kidnapped and tortured. Really put the fear of God in me."

"God?" she laughed as she asked in a mocking way. "Not exactly what I was going for anyways, lover." I turned and twisted in the forest, trying to find the source of the voice.

"Why don't we cut the shit and just come out into the open? We both know the end game here." I was starting to back track to the opening, watching over my shoulder and as many angles around me as I could in case she came flying in. As I made it back to where the witches had the fire, I heard her loud cackle as thunder struck high in the night sky, and then heard her voice, strong and clear, behind me.

"Hi, Cole." She was standing about 10 yards from me, glaring.

"Fuck you. No offense." I said with a sarcastic grin. My hand was on my bone handle knife. I have been waiting on this moment. *I'm itching to kill this thing.*

"Oh, big talk for a guy in over his head." She grinned as she floated into the air and shot her arms out to the side, sending lightning through the air from her fingertips. The ground shook with fear and anticipation. I gripped the handle of my knife waiting on my opportunity. Then, confusion washed over her face, the lightning died down, and she looked at me from her perch in the sky.

"Not quite what you expected is it?" I smiled at her as I began to figure out what was going on. She started floating back to the earth, looking at me with great distain.

"Where are they?" she screamed as her feet hit the ground.

"Oh, you mean the thirty or so devil worshiping old hags who you thought would have caught and killed me by now? Yeah they're dead. I killed them." Her face was twitching with rage.

"Impossible."

"No, it's true. You see, I wanted them to chase me. I tricked them into running into a trap pit and impaling themselves on some sharpened branches while you spent your time killing Blake." She let out a banshee like scream in disbelief of my statement.

"You'll pay for what you've done to the coven you insignificant human." She was squaring me up, keeping herself from attacking me right now.

"I respectfully disagree. I think, judging by the oh shit look on your face, you were counting on strength in numbers to take me out. Well, your bitches are burning in a hole right now. And I think I am significant, or at least you and your boss thought I was at some point. Either way, you'll remember my name."

"Why is that?" she growled.

"Because I'm going to kill you." She dug her back foot into the dirt and squatted low, readying to come after me. I winked and grinned as she took off in a sprint in my direction, screaming the whole way. I stood frozen in my spot, waiting for the right time. She got within five feet and leapt at me, eyes glowing red and hands reaching for my neck. When I felt her hands grab onto my neck, I grabbed her shoulder with my right hand, pulling her in tight as I fell to my back. I put my feet into her pelvis and began to roll back. Simultaneously, I pulled my knife with my left hand, burying the long blade deep into her rib cage.

We rolled back together, and with a swift kick I sent her flying over me, twisting my knife and pulling down as I did. Her blood covered me as she landed hard on the ground behind me, tumbling end over end a few times. I got up to go after her. She was crawling away slowly, contorting her body in an inhuman way. She spun her head backwards like an owl, flashing her glowing red eyes at me, and flaring wolfe like yellow fangs as she snarled viciously. I picked a log up out of the fire, making sure it was still aflame on one end. I wiped the blood from my eyes as I closed in on her from behind.

I took one boot and pushed her down to the dirt. She cried in agony and rage. I thrust the log fireside first into her back, pinning her to the floor. She let out one last ear piercing scream as I leaned in, pushing her head back into the dirt. I pulled my axe off my back and brought the blade around next to her face so she could see it.

"Listen, bitch, I told you this would happen. From the night you decided to try and take my will, I knew it would end this way." She was kicking up dirt and blood as she breathed hard. I leaned in to whisper in her ear, "I just wanted you to know before I cut off your head and throw your body in the pit with the rest of them, this one is for Ty." I moved away and turned the axe blade, getting ready to behead her. Then, I moved back in for one last thought. "Oh, and by the way, Thanks for that night. It really was something." I laughed in her ear and then hopped to my feet, swinging my axe up and over my shoulders. She was moaning in fear on the ground below me. Anger washed over me as I rotated the axe and thrust down with all my force, cutting clean through the bone and spinal cord with one swing.

Sticking her body onto the blade of my axe, I drug her back through the woods to the impaling trap pit I had made. It was quiet now, and the fire was below the side walls, but the smell of rotting human flesh still filled the air. I pried her off of my axe and rolled her body into the pit. The flames shot up as if I had thrown a container of gasoline in. For a second relief came over me. Part of me wanted to stay there and watch that fire the rest of the night. I felt as if a hundred pounds of led was finally off my chest. Quickly though, thoughts of Katie filled my brain and I became more focused than ever.

As I walked from the pit back through the woods to the first clearing, I came across Elaine's head. It was lying there motionless, mouth agape, and eyes still glowing red. The more I thought about what she had done, and the more I thought about Katie, the more pissed off I became. I bent down, grabbing the disembodied head by the hair and carried it along with me.

Axe in one hand, disembodied head in the other, I made my way further into the woods looking for the men in charge of the coven. Looking for Katie.

"C'mon you dirty bastards! I'm right here!" I was walking with purpose, following the sounds of that ominous flute. "Come and see what I did to your little errand girl." I was shaking with anger. As I walked further into the woods, the sound of the music waned, and the sounds of the night proved more sinister. I was coming up on another clearing, and in the shadows I can see the figure of a man. I stop, but before I can address him, he speaks to me.

"We've been waiting on you, Cole." A voice stated from the direction of the shadow figure. I knew that voice. It was impossible to forget. The smugness radiated from it unfathomably. It was Kevin Walker.

"Kevin Walker?" I asked rhetorically. "Well hell, I should have known you were in on this." Kevin laughed as he stepped from the shadows into the moonlight. He was dressed in a dark robe, with a deep hood covering the majority of his face.

"Now why would you say that Cole, because of Elaine?"

"Damn right because of Elaine. She must have got all your crazy. Like uncle, like cunt I always say." Kevin's eyes lit up with fire at the way I talked about her.

"Cole," he said between chuckles, "there's just so much you don't know yet."

"What more do I need to know? You introduced your only niece to a coven and groomed her to be as sorry as you. Black and white to me."

"It's more than that, Cole. Not only did I groom her from a young age, but I sacrificed her to Lilith. I sacrificed her to be the vessel." My face wrinkled in disgust at that statement. Even someone like her didn't deserve that.

"You people. I just don't get it. All this work, sacrificing your own family to appease something evil in these woods. And after all that, after a lifetime of work and planning, I'm just going to kill you anyways." Kevin pulled back the hood from his face, his eyes glossed over black as he laughed harder at me.

"You are going to kill me? Cole, I'm sorry son, but you're nothing more than a failure. You always have been." My body tensed as anger again washed over me. I never liked this guy, but now I *hate* him.

"Maybe things have changed, Kevin. There's only one way to find out." I gripped my axe and prepared myself to walk in the clearing after him.

"You're right. There is one way we can find out. Or maybe we can look at the facts. You couldn't save Tyler. Fail.

Not only could you not save Elaine, you spited her, then had sex with her before finding out she was the root of your problems. Fail."

"Is this going anywhere?" I interrupted sarcastically.

"You couldn't save Katie," he said with a grin. "Fail." With a wave of his hand, a great light shone into the clearing, revealing a big inverted cross made from the timber of the woods. And on the cross, there hung Katie. Her mutilated body hung lifeless on the upside down cross, while her innards made for a kind of morbid garland across her limp corpse.

My heart ripped from my chest and hit the floor. Tears involuntarily ran down my cheeks. I could feel Kevin looking on at me in satisfaction. I lowered my head, partially in an attempt to regain myself, and mostly because I couldn't stand the sight any longer. Then, I slowly raised my head and a grin formed on my face.

"I'll tell you one thing I *didn't* fail at, you smug son of a bitch."

"What's that, boy?" he shouted confidently at me.

"I'm the one who killed your precious Lilith." Shock filled the face of Kevin followed by disbelief as I stepped out from the dark shadows of the woods into the clearing, rolling Elaine's head across the ground towards his feet.

Kevin's body began to tremble as he bent down to touch the head of his former niece. What was a minute ago a powerful man with a grand presentation of evil quickly had turned into a fragile shell with only a soft whimper coming from it.

"No! No! It isn't supposed to be this way!" He cried as he held the decapitated head in his hands. I had walked up to him now. He was completely broken, sunk onto the ground defeated.

"I just need you to tell me one thing Kevin. Tell me one thing before I send you to hell with her." He looked up at me, eyes filled with pain.

"What is it?"

"Did you have anything to do with that?" I pointed the blade of my axe at the cross, still unable to look in her direction.

"No." He sulked. "I was just supposed to present it to you. I was supposed to break your spirit. The man you are looking for is Addison Miller."

"Addison Miller. Well, I promise you, I *will* find him. And I will make damn sure that I take my sweet, sweet time picking him apart limb from limb." Kevin began to break down and sob loudly. I took my axe into both hands, preparing to lift it overhead. I laid the axe across one arm as I used the other to clinch Kevin's head and pull back by the hair. He winced and his lip quivered with fear of what I was about to do. He was right to be afraid. "Tell Elaine I said hi." I whispered in his ear as I swung the axe high above my head. Kevin let out a ghastly scream as I swung down and buried the blade deep between his eyes.

I placed a foot on the chest of Kevin and wedged the blade of my axe out, kicking his lifeless corpse to the ground. My body began to involuntarily shake as I remembered that the love of my life was hanging high in the corner, cold and limp. Tears fell swift from my eyes. Losing her was the most surreal pain I had ever felt in my life. Worse than losing Ty, worse than anything

Elaine or any of these evil fuckers in these woods could try and do to break me. Katie had the power to wash away everything bad that had ever happen to me. All she had to do was be there. Even when she was yelling at me, something about her just made life bearable. She was all that I had left.

After a few minutes of standing in that clearing sobbing, a truly evil rage came over me. My face began to twitch. Control was quickly slipping away from me. I could feel myself begin to lift my axe over my head again, but it felt more like I was outside of my body, watching from a distance. The axe began to hammer down into the dead body of Kevin Walker, mangling what was left of him horribly. I was numb. The bones of his body began to break, and what was once a human being began to in places have the consistency of a holiday gelatin dish. Over and over again the blade of my axe smashed into his corpse, and a smirk emerged underneath the splatters of blood on my face. I didn't stop burying the axe into him until what was left was a mixure of bone fragment and mush, and what lie beneath me was unrecognizable as a human.

I put the axe down as exhaustion stopped me from continuing. Breathing heavy I stood there looking at my handy work, face still twitching uncontrollably. I thought back on John. I thought about how nurturing he was with me and easing me in to this mess. He never wanted this life for me, but he knew who I was. *Who I was meant to be.* I thought about Katie and how she wouldn't want me to stop now. She wouldn't want me to walk away in consumed with grief, and she wouldn't want me to kill Addison Miller in the name of revenge. Tears once again streamed down my face as I remembered how beautiful both of them were. This was bigger than me. Bigger than justice for them or Ty. There was a responsibility in play for me to cleanse this town of its evil. They were counting on a hero. Whether I like it or not, *I am that hero.*

The rage inside me was still burning bright, however the control was back. I was me again. I picked up my axe and gripped it tight as I began to trek deeper into the woods looking for my target.

"Addison Miller!" I screamed through tears of raw emotion, "Come out and face me you yellow coward!" Thunder rolled loud overhead and the air filled with a chill. "I know you're here, you son of a bitch! Let's see how bad you are. Face to face." Rain began to come down in sheets as the thunder rolled ominously. The sound of a flute playing began to float on the wind through the trees. Then suddenly, a gust of wind blew past me, the flute died down, and a bolt of lighting Flashed and struck about fifty feet in front of me. From behind the flash of lighting, out stepped Addison Miller. He was cloaked in a dark hooded robe. His eyes shone red, and his face was deathly pale. As he stepped towards me, I noticed that there were not feet under his robe, but hooves. Whatever he was, it wasn't human.

"So, you figured me out. Congratulations, Cole. I'm quite surprised you've made it this far honestly." Addison's voice was accompanied by others, growling and moaning in unison with his regular voice as he talked. A putrid smell of rotting flesh radiated off of him as he stood in front of me.

"I've figured out more than you think, I'm sure of that." I could feel my face twitching with rage as I responded to this monster. Addison leaned back and let out a manically arrogant laugh in all his multiple voices, and it rang loud through the forest trees.

"Whatever you think you know, son, there's plenty of doors you haven't opened." Addison snarled as he tried to burn a hole through me with those glowing red eyes. It looked as though he was trying to figure me out; trying to see if I was intimidated.

"I may not know everything Addison, but what I do know is this coven is a lot bigger than our little town, and you want to keep the expansion rolling." A grin appeared on his face as I was talking. "And it's funny you mention doors, because from where I sit, the doors that are closed are sealed, and that's because of my father, so they should stay that way. Even in death, he still has one over on you, doesn't he?" I smirked as I watched the distain wash over his face.

"Whatever helps you sleep at night."

"I'll tell you what will help me sleep at night, Addison. Adding a notch in my belt for killing you, just the same as I killed all your little helpers here tonight." His grin became more shallow, and I was starting to see through the façade. The expression on his face gave away his unsurety, and I could tell what he was questioning in his mind. *Did I really kill all those witches here tonight? Where was Kevin, or Elaine?* His malicious mind games of intimidation and self-loathing were losing traction. His grip was waning. I could *feel* it.

"You've killed nothing!" The voices shouted angrily. Addison was foaming from the mouth, spitting and snarling uncontrollably. "We have a plan in place," the voices continued, "You cannot stop us. Nobody can. For we are *Legion*."

"You may be Legion. Maybe you *had* a plan. I promise you, you evil sack of shit, that I will not let it happen. No matter how many contingents or plan B's I have to sludge through, and I don't care if I have to slaughter a million of you son's a bitches, I will *never* let you win." I was shaking with intensity. I began to ready myself for what inevitably lied ahead. Addison stepped towards me, hissing like a serpent. My hands readied over my axe, waiting for the right time to make their move. Just as Addison began to move towards me, a bolt of lightning shot down from the sky and hit directly between us. Sparks and smoke filled the space between us. I fell to the ground disoriented, my vision blurry. Trying to collect myself, I frantically looked around for Addison, but he was nowhere. Then, a high pitched, blood curdling scream filled my ears. My eyes began to go black. The scream was surrounding me. I am losing control of my body as my vision becomes darker and darker. This was it, he was winning.

Everyone's Hero

The world was starting to come back to me now. I'm not sure how long it's been since I lost consciousness, but I can draw one conclusion, it was all Addison's doing. As my bearings began to come back to me, I noticed that I was no longer laying on the ground, but on a raised alter, directly in the middle of the clearing. My wrists and ankles were tied, and there were candles all around my body. I had become the sacrificial lamb.

"Welcome to the party, sleepy head!" Addison's sinister and deep voice bellowed from just in front of me. I could lift my head enough to see him standing there, red eyes glaring from underneath the hood of his robe. I could hear shifting around me, like there were other people watching, but I couldn't move enough to see who—or what, it was. I was speechless. I was defeated.

"Aw, come one, don't go silent on me again! " he started again, "This is just starting to get fun!" The sound of the flute that had led me into the lions den was back. I would like to say that it sounded evil, or ominous, or ghoulish, but it was beautiful. It was captivating. Addison was looking over me from the foot of the alter, rolling his fingers in a motion from his pinky to his index finger, tapping his vampiricly long nails on the alter top. "Where's the kid who was telling me something about my plan that he was going to squander? I miss that spunk. It makes this all the more enjoyable." A high pitched voice from inside Addison laughed in the background at what the deeper voice had to say. The smell protruding off of him was putrid.

"Well, that particular kid is a little tied up right now, he'll have to get back with you." I winced as I tried to adjust my hands and feet under the rope. "So what is the plan now, huh? You couldn't convince me to kill myself, even after all that you tried, so you're just going to kill me now and say fuck it?" Addison snarled in disgust at my remarks.

"There's always a backup plan." The voices announced. "By now it's obvious that you know about the seals, and why we are trying to break them."

"Yeah, your crazy small town ass is trying to open the door to the damn devil."

"Smart boy," Addison smiled, bearing sharp predator like teeth as he continued, "But, Lucifer wasn't the only piece to the puzzle. I'll be honest with you Cole, what you did to 'Elaine' really put a damper on our big plans."

"You mean that Lilith thing? Yeah, sorry about that. Turns out she wasn't as clever as she thought."

"Hold your tongue, you peasant!" Addison growled at me in distain. "Lilith is the first, she is our queen.

"I slit her from her gut to her gullet," I stated as I raised an eyebrow and smirked, "It wasn't even a fight!" I was full blown laughing at him now, keeping an eye to see if I was provoking him.

"Shut your cunting mouth you maggot!" he screamed. He was gripping the edge of the alter hard enough to tear it off.

"Oh," I started again, "I almost left out the best part. After I gutted her like a pig, I cut her damn head off with my axe and threw her body in a pit to burn with the rest of your whores."

Addison let out a roar as he leapt toward me in a flying motion, landing beside my head. With a swift movement, he sliced into my cheek and mouth with his nails. The stinging was white hot and I could taste the blood on my lips.

"I am the Shepard." Addison stated. My mouth began to fill with blood from the laceration on my face. He slid his nail down my neck to my chest, pressing just hard enough to draw blood. I felt a venom like sting coursing through my body as he continued his speech.

"This town made a deal a long time ago. A deal to keep a dying, miserable little town prospering during hard times. And that deal was to give up every first-born son, for 40 years. At the end of those 40 years, a chosen one will be born. He would be a prodigy; successful in every venture. This child was to be groomed into a leader, so that he could fufill the plan and accept Lucifer into him. This is the plan. This is the *word*. This is the pact."

"So, that kid was you, huh?" I gurgled and spit up my own blood as I tried to raise my head and continue. "You're the

Shepard. Well, I'm glad to hear it. It's a shame that you don't have a flock anymore though. My bad on that one." Addison let out a deep growl as he dug each finger of his hand into my stomach. I screamed in agony as he wrenched and tore at my flesh.

"You're right, Cole." He stated as he twisted his hand and dug even deeper into my skin. "You did slaughter my flock. You spoiled what was supposed to be an easy plan time and *time* again!" I could feel my consciousness waning. Blood bubbled and spattered from my nose and mouth as I tried to murmur something. "The thing is," he continued, "You staying alive was never *really* vital to the end game." I could feel my body trembling now. I feel weak, cold. "You see, oh righteous one, you killing yourself certainly *would* have opened the seal. But, there are other ways around that." A rank smell filled the air as Addison got closer to me and smiled from ear to ear. "I'll show you what I mean."

Suddenly, lightning struck about 10 yards from the alter, and a fire started to burn brightly. Then, out of the shadows of the woods, a figure started walking towards the fire holding something above its head.

"You see, while you are a son of a righteous man, you are not *the* son of said righteous man." *What the hell was he talking about? I have a brother?* "That's right, Cole. There's actually three of you. One you killed back there in the forest. And this one, holding your pride and joy." Addison laughed hysterically as he motioned for the man to move closer and reveal himself and whatever he was holding.

The world began to spin through my eyes and light headedness overtook me. I managed to lift my head to try and concentrate on who was walking towards me. As he stepped into the light, I quickly realized I knew who this was. It was Damien Johnson, a new transfer to the school this year, and he was holding a *baby*. The world around me was fading out slowly. This was it. The coven had won.

"Let up a little Addison, I want him conscious for this part at least." The arrogant voice of Damien filled my ears. Within seconds, the pressure let up in my stomach, and a breath of life filled my lungs, shocking me awake for the time being. I looked over my left shoulder, and there stood Damien, holding a newborn child in his hands. "See this?" he continued, "This is the start of our new flock, Cole. This is *your* child."

"What the hell are you talking about?" I murmured through nausea and bloody saliva.

"Allow me to explain," he stated. "You see, you meeting up with Elaine that night was supposed to break you. You were supposed to die that night."

"Sorry to burst your bubble, bro." My words were met with and intense pain as Addison dug his nails deep into my wounds to silence me.

"Don't interrupt him you little prick!" he growled.

"As I was saying," Damien started again with a smirk, "You were *supposed* to kill yourself. That was not the only plan, however. Your old man was a step behind us, as usual."

"Don't talk about him like that, you Wizard of Oz reject."

"Oh, Cole" Damien said with a laugh, "I think I'm more qualified to talk about dear old dad than you. Anywho, as you will soon find out, there is *always* a contingent plan in place. Elaine was given specific instructions to not only try to mentally break you, but to get you to impregnate her. Cole, you impregnated a demon. Do you have any idea how special this child is?"

"Well if he gets my looks, I'd say he's pretty damn special."

"You can be a smartass all you want, but the fear is imminent on your face." He was right. *What the fuck did I do? Why was I ever there in the first place? I should have known better.* "Cole, you may have put a damper on things tonight, but you certainly didn't ruin anything. Your child can be the chosen one. He can rebuild our coven. He can summon Lucifer."

"So without further ado, I'd like to get on to the part where I rid the coven of this pest of a man, thank you very much." Addison smirked proudly as the wind shifted and began to blow violently across my body. I didn't feel pain anymore. My body was going numb and all sensations were waning. I wanted to give in. I was ready for it to be over. I lost again.

Suddenly, an enormous gust of wind accompanied by a radiant white light smacked into Addison with a godly force. I could feel his nails pull out of my body. I could tell something had collided with him and sent him reeling. A warm sensation was slowly rising up my body from my feet to my chest. *Something had joined us.*

"Stand up, Cole." A voice rang out, in a firm but comforting tone. I raised my head as far as I could manage trying to locate the voice. It was instantly recognizable. That voice could soothe me no matter what state I was in, current one included. I fell in love with that voice. It was Katie.

"Katie?" that question escaped me aloud as I began to question my sanity.

"Cole, it's me. Stand up, it's time for you to be a hero." *I must really be dead this time.* The thought of my dead girlfriend being alive or a spirit or something right in front of me isn't fathomable.

"Katie, I can't see you. And I can't get up. I think I'm dying" *Was I talking to myself? If this is real, why can't I see her?*

"You aren't dying, Cole. You can stand. I need you to get up." I could feel her breathe on my face. I can smell her perfume.

"Katie, I'm in bad shape, I'm afraid to stand up. I need to see you." My heart was racing again. I wanted to stand up, but what good will I be against them? Addison turned my stomach into swiss cheese.

"The Cole I know never showed fear." I could picture the smile on her face as she spoke those words. She was right, I'm not one to admit fear so readily. *But was I still that guy?* "Cole, if you stand up, you'll see me." A sensation of light filled my limbs as I wearily lifted my battered body off of the alter and stood up next to it. A wonderfull white illumination was gleaming in front of me. I knew it was her. I was not aware of Addison or

Damien, my surroundings were silent. I felt at total peace. Finally, out of the light she appeared to me. A tear softly fell down my cheek as I felt her grab ahold of my hands and fill the hole in my heart.

"Cole," she continued, "I know you're tired. You've been through so much. But it's time for you to rise up." I could feel my hands start to become steady from the strength in her grip. Tears continued to flow from my eyes as she spoke to me. "Cole, so many people are counting on you. You're family was chosen for a reason. John believed in you for a reason, and so did I." She leaned in and I felt a gentle kiss on my forehead. "Don't let my death be in vain. Know that I'll be with you always. Be strong, Cole. Goodbye."

I smiled between the tears as her hands slipped through mine and Katie faded back into the light. She had left me, but this time, I didn't feel like she was gone. I could feel my blood pumping and adrenaline coursing through me as I spotted Addison lying in the corner of the clearing. It was just us two now, and he was looking up cowardly at me like a dog that's just peed on the living room floor. All fear and pain had left me. I noticed my hickory axe lying about ten yards in front of me, but I focused my eyes on Addison as he slowly started to stir.

"Cole, I know what you're thinking and it doesn't have to be this way you know." Addison began his lowly pitch to me as he straightened his stance.

"And what way is that?" I took a few deliberate steps toward my axe. I could feel his eyes dancing up and down my position as I crept closer to his demise.

"Cole, you don't know the whole story." He continued, "I could fill you in. Haven't you been wondering why your mother chose us, and your estranged father is supposedly the hero of this story?" Addison shot an insincere smile my way as he tried to spin his web.

"Addison," I started as I moved closer to the axe and focused my attention directly on him like a hawk, "That kind of pathetic reach for an escape would probably work on a lesser man." The smile was withering away rather quickly from his face now. "See, there's a big part of your story that doesn't hit home for me. Of course I've wondered about my mother, and why she was the villan, and a father I never knew was a supposed good guy out here fighting the good fight. I wondered how my mother could be so bad given that I knew my grandfather and he is the greatest person I've ever known." Confusion draped the face of Addison as he wondered what direction I was heading in. "But you see, what I do know is John might have been abscent in my life, but she wasn't present either. I just thought it was because she was sick. Turns out she was nothing but a sick follower of a weak man like you."

"I'm no man!" Addison growled defensively in my direction.

"Absolutely, my mistake." I smiled as my boots were now touching the handle of the axe. "Let's not jump ahead of ourselves quite yet though. You see Addison, you were tugging at me a little, trying to bring up my past, and bring up John to distract me, but one flaw in your sales pitch was you got the hero part wrong."

"What do you mean?" he asked unassumingly. Fear was covering him as he stood there awaiting my next move.

"You said John was the supposed to be the hero of this story. That's where you fucked up." Addison's dark eyes widened. He knew what was approaching. "You fucked up in this aspect from the start. What you never realized is *I'm* the hero of this story. And you, you son of a bitch, well you're nothing more than my last victory."

Addison let out a devlish cry as he extended both arms horizontally and hovered across the ground in my direction. I quickly bent down and retrieved my axe. Confidence radiated through my body. But not only confidence. Accompanying that feeling was an overshadowing rage. I felt deep hatred for this man. *This thing.* Simply killing him would not be enough. *I needed to make it count.*

As Addison neared me, I buried my boot deep into his sternum, knocking him backwards and onto the ground. He slammed hard into the ground and rolled backward, letting out a groan. Before he could regain footing I was above him, and met his face with the butt end of my axe. He shrieked as the blow put his head into the dirt. I dropped the axe to my side and knelt down slowly, relishing in the moment I was about to have. I straddled Addison's wounded body, and with my right hand I forced him to look up at me. With a grin, I hooked a left into his face with every ounce of force I could muster. I could feel his face give way to my clenched fist and hit the ground hard. I've never felt more content than I did in this moment. Feelings of pride and gluttony took me over. *I was winning. I was getting my revenge. I wanted more.*

Revenge consumed me as I thrust one hard fist after another into the face of Addison. I can feel bones breaking underneath my knuckles. The sound soothed me. The warm sensation of his blood against my hand was a sort of validation for me that everything I had gone through was worth it. I felt the long bony hands of Addison reaching up towards me, pleading with me to cease-fire. It only fueled me to continue.

Blow after blow, sounds of crackling bones and gargling over body fluids turned into a sound more consistant with me hitting a ripe fruit as opposed to the face of another man.

Something about this accompanied with the ominous silence of Addison prompted me to stop. *It was time to finish the job.*

I stood up and grabbed my axe from beside us, standing over the mangled body of my antagonist. As he clawed at my feet, reaching out for any chance of escape from his fate, I thought of Ty. I thought about how my best friend was taken from this world from no fault of his own. Solely to get at me, he was killed. I thought about John. My whole childhood I hated the thought of my father. He was absent from my life. I learned everything I needed to know from my grandfather. I considered him my real dad. But then I met John, and shortly there after found a way to truly respect this man and look up to him in a way. I thought about how his life was ended. All of his work cut short before he could see the fruits of his labor. Before he could see me, and how I'm now who I'm meant to be. He was killed because of me.

Then, as I spun the axe in my hands, I thought about Katie. I thought about how despite all of our issues, she was it. She pulled me from the ledge, *twice.* I thought about how much I was going to miss her once this was over. My lip began to quiver as my emotions were once again taking over. I began to think about her plea to me, that I 'stand up and be a hero.' That's what this was about. It wasn't glamorous, and I'm definitely not perfect, but I *have* to be a hero. I grabbed firmly ahold of the handle and looked down upon my target. He was doing his best to grovel, but his body was making that an insurmountable feat.

I squatted down and shifted the axe into one hand, grasping a handful of scalp and hair with the other, forcing him to look at me. Carnage is an understatement for the swollen and macabre state of the face starting up at me. I grinned as I leaned in close and whispered, "I want you to know that your life hangs in my hands. You should have never underestimated me." I could feel hairs detaching from his head at the root as I tightened my grip, wrenching his head farther back as I continued, "Everything you had done to me to try to break me, it motivated me. Like I told you before, *I'm* the hero of this story. And that's because of you." I shoved his motionless head back into the ground and exploded upwards, grabbing the axe again with both hands; pivoting at the hips and converting that explosion through the axe in a downward motion, colliding viciously with his skull. The blow forced the

sharpened maul to slice strait through flesh and bone and bury

itself in the ground below.

I stepped on the sternum, leveraging the axe back out

of the ground and out of his head while his arms and feet twitched

at random around me. I stepped back, taking in everything that

had happened over the coarse of the night, and dropping the axe I

fell to my knees, overcome with exhausting emotion. A soft rain

began to fall from the night sky, accompanied by a dull, gentle

thunder. The pressure of what I just had to do was finally off of

me. The pressure of a whole town was off of my shoulders. I

wasn't able to move, I just knelt here, letting it all go.

Once I felt I was able to move, I began to stand up and

try to piece together my next move. I'm not sure that my life can

ever go back to some semblance of what it was before all of this,

and I'm not sure I'd want it to. Despite everything I've gone

through, tonight I did what had to be done. I reached my full

potential. And if Addison was right about any of this, it was that I don't know the whole story. I think figuring that out is a good

place to start.

The End

Made in the USA
Monee, IL
13 March 2020

23102749R00134